Francis B Nyamnjoh
Stories from Abakwa
Mind Searching
The Disillusioned African
The Convert
Souls Forgotten

Dibussi Tande
No Turning Back. Poems of Fre

Kangsen Feka Wakai
Fragmented Melodies

Ntemfac Ofege
Namondo. Child of the Water Spirit

Emmanuel Fru Doh
Not Yet Damascus

Thomas Jing
Tale of an African Woman

Peter Wuteh Vakunta
Grassfields Stories from Cameroon

Ba'bila Mutia
Coils of Mortal Flesh

Kehbuma Langmia
Titabet and The Takumbeng

Ngessimo Mathe Mutaka
Building Capacity: Using TEFL and African languages as development-oriented literacy tools

Milton Krieger
Cameroon's Social Democratic Front: Its History and Prospects as an Opposition Political party, 1990-2011

Sammy Oke Akombi
The Woman Who Ate Python & Other Stories

Susan Nkwentie Nde
Precipice

Francis B Nyamnjoh & Richard Fonteh Akum
The GCE Crisis: A Test of Anglophone Solidarity

THE RAPED AMULET

Sammy Oke Akombi

***Langaa* Research & Publishing CIG**
Mankon, Bamenda

Publisher:
Langaa RPCIG
(*Langaa* Research & Publishing Common Initiative Group)
P.O. Box 902 Mankon
Bamenda
North West Province
Cameroon
Langaagrp@gmail.com
www.langaapublisher.com

ISBN:9956-558-24-9

DISCLAIMER
All views expressed in this publication are those of the author and do not necessarily reflect the views of Langaa RPCIG.

Content

Chapter One   1

Chapter Two   7

Chapter Three   12

Chapter Four   17

Chapter Five   31

Chapter Six   37

Chapter Seven   47

Chapter Eight   53

Chapter Nine   62

Chapter Ten   68

Chapter Eleven   78

Chapter Twelve   88

Chapter Thirteen   100

Chapter Thirteen   108

ion Ekpochaba rubbed his eyes gently, sighed and then rolled in his bed from one side to another. He opened the eyes and then closed them again, It was not unusual for him to remain wrapped up in a duvet for long hours on a Sunday morning. But fortunes seemed to have changed. For two straight weeks he had been bugged down by assignments and reading lists. They had kept streaming onto his hands like rivulets from the highlands of Mandara. In order to avoid being drowned by them, he had to work hard in order to kill his old habits. He had to come to terms with the fact that he was no longer the master of his own activities, dictating and directing their pace and path as he wished. He had become an occupant of one of the thirty-four sitting places in a lecture room in far away University of Warwick in Coventry of the English Midlands, in quest of a diploma. There, he was anxiously taking down notes from other teachers instead of dictating them for others as he had been used to doing.

Reluctantly, Dion pulled out his five feet eight inches out of the warmth of his bed and went to the toilets. After he had brushed his teeth he decided to go to the kitchen, where he found his flat mates who were already having their breakfast. Cooking had never been his strong point ever since he was born, twenty-eight years ago. He could only vaguely remember the number of times he had entered the kitchen – only a few times, probably ten times. He had grown up

1

in an environment where boys had nothing to do with the kitchen. A father usually got terribly agitated on finding his son in the kitchen. 'What in the name of my maternal ancestry are you doing there?' he would bellow. 'Would you get out of there, with immediate effect!'

Dion had always known the kitchen to be the exclusive reserve of the womenfolk. His father had always pulled his ears and told him that women had been made for only three things: kids, kitchen and church and the rest of the things were for men. But the present time had taught him that he had to face the kitchen squarely. He got a mug, put in some water and then some fresh milk and a Lipton tea bag. He opened the microwave oven and placed the mug in it. He set it accordingly and in about one and half minute his mug of tea was ready. He put five slices of bread in a toaster and shortly after, Dion was having his breakfast.

When he returned to his room, it was to bend over books. Books! Yes books. They had become his main companions. They were really many. Fat ones, plump ones, stout ones, skinny ones and even senile ones. He had to accept them all because he had come to England for their sake. He had forsaken everything that had made him proud and happy in order to run after them. This had rendered him a sojourner in an alien land and he had become infected with the worrying syndrome that was typical of school boys and girls – worrying about completing the assignment, worrying about the presentation, the next evaluation, improving on the previous mark, library research, pleasing the teacher etc. One after the other he flipped through the resentful pages of the different books, scribbling notes and occasionally trying to let some facts stick in his head. Having sat down for four hours, he felt an urge to stop. He tried in vain to resist, so he got up and just then a rumble ran through his stomach. He understood the signal and thought about facing the awful kitchen again. He closed the book whose pages were still staring at him and went to the kitchen. This time there was none of his flat mates in it. He opened the common refrigerator and took out a packet of sausages from his stock. Before he closed it his eyes caught the inscription "No scoffing" on the food provisions of one of the mates, an English boy who seemed to be so busy with his own business that he hardly returned the hellos of his flat mates. It was the first time Dion had come across the word scoffing. He wondered what it meant. The food provisions of this young man had been carefully wrapped up in transparent plastic material and then labelled no scoffing. Dion closed the refrigerator and went back to his room, picked up a dictionary and looked up the word scoffing. The word meant different things and it was difficult to decide on the one the young man meant. The context was food preserved in a common refrigerator. The meaning that was close to that context was to eat eagerly and fast. Did it mean that someone in the flat had been eagerly eating up Mathew's (so the English boy was called) food provision? The message it conveyed to Dion was that nobody should touch his stuff, which was unnecessary because everyone in the flat was responsible. He found the inscription belittling, which anyway was another meaning of scoffing. He thought he should discuss the matter with Mathew, he was a difficult person to talk to, though.

Dion took out four sausages from the pack and put them in a dish. He then defrosted some potato chips and joined them with the sausages. He placed them in a grill and in ten minutes his lunch was ready. After he had eaten he drank a pint of apple juice. He had conquered the hunger in him but he still hungered for dishes like *ekwang, koki,* and *ebvai neh eru.* All the same, Dion went back to his books. He worked again for three hours and decided to take a break. He realized that the sun, instead of reducing in intensity as it was getting late in the day, was rather growing more intense. It imposed its rays on the city of Coventry. A name that reminded Dion of his secondary school days when he and his girlfriend were sent to Coventry and nobody wanted to speak to them or make friends with them. They were isolated for almost a month and this affected their studies very much. After that he had never approved that anyone be sent to Coventry and had inwardly vowed never to have anything to do with Coventry. And then fate had decided to put him right in the heart of Coventry. After a very cold night in London he had to take a train the following day to Coventry of all places. Dion had no other choice but to disavow his previous vow against Coventry. He took a fast train and in a matter of hours he was in the beautiful city of Coventry. At the railway station

4

he took a taxi to Warwick University, which was a few kilometres away. The layout of the city made him wonder if he had not suddenly found himself in a most exquisite garden city. Thank God he had disavowed his vow. That was a place to be. He was so carried away by the beauty that he did not realize he was at his destination. The taxi driver announced, "buddy, here we are. This is the central campus of Warwick University."

"How much is the fare?" Dion asked him.

"I suppose you can read," he said coldly.

"Yes of course, I have come here just for that reason," he replied.

"Then read the meter" he said impatiently.

"Oh the meter, where is it"? Dion inquired.

The cab driver indicated the meter with his hand and Dion read twelve pounds. He counted twelve pounds and gave the driver, took out his luggage and went looking for the registration office. Twelve pounds was the equivalent of about eight thousand francs, an amount that one pays as fare, back in his country, for a journey of over a thousand kilometres. Dion shook his head vigorously, wondering whether he was going to cope with such expensive lifestyle. Well, he never took a taxi again.

He found the registration office and the keys to his room at Tocil flats were waiting only for the asking. That was quite a while ago.

Dion Ekpochaba thought of bending over his books again but there was an unsettling urge that kept his mind away from them. He decided to lie on his bed and let the urge fade away, but he still felt restive and so he made up his mind to go out for a walk. He wore his shoes and jumpers and was set to step out of his room but he struck his left foot against the rubber doorstop fixed to the wall. "What an ominous sign," he thought. He sat back on his bed and sank into deep contemplation. He wondered whether he should change his mind about going out that day but the urge to go out had the better of him and that sent him to thinking about an amulet that had been handed to him by the elders of his family before he travelled to the U.K. He reached for his suitcase which he had kept at the top of his wardrobe and brought it down. He unzipped it and fished out the amulet. It was a bloated object of raw leather material, carefully sewn up. It measured about half an inch in length and a quarter of an inch in diameter. It had a black string attached to it, letting it be worn around the neck. He kissed it and wore it around his neck. That was the amulet – the great protector of persons from impending evil. No one born of Dion's tribe would venture far away from their homeland without taking along an amulet.

hen it had become certain that Dion Ekpochaba would be travelling to the United Kingdom for further studies, it was incumbent upon him to inform every member of his extended family. Majority of them were duly informed – uncles, aunts, brothers, sisters, cousins, and even in-laws. They all recognized that it was a great honour to have them informed about an event as important as that. It was not unusual for any family to savour such an event only once in a lifetime, so it was arranged that the entire family should meet in the village - home of the ancestors, the living and the dead. Dion had always wondered about a situation during which his entire family would meet because of him. He knew for sure that it would happen during his wedding, which has been overdue and of course during his death. Only he would not be part of them for the latter, so he used to look forward only to the former. Well, another occasion had surprisingly come up and he could feel his own importance swelling up, around him. All the people were all praise for him and they hoped that he was the window on the world for the entire family. They hoped that other family members would follow his example. The evening was a very special one, an elaborate family meeting was held, during which the family history was told and the younger members got to know that their family had been one of the most prominent families of that village but somehow

7

death and irresponsibility had weakened it and some people in the village had been taking advantage of the situation. Thanks to the ongoing event, an appeal was made to all the members to sit up and bring back its past glories. It would start by ensuring that their son, Dion Ekpochaba, travelled safely to the United Kingdom. There was so much to eat and drink that the people went to bed only in the very small hours of the following day.

At six a.m. they were up again, gathered in the house of the head of the family. They went behind the house and sat down in a horse-shoe formation. There were thirty-six family members in all. The family head sat on a low stool in front of them. Between his legs a small hole had been dug and at his left side were the following items: a black cock whose legs had been tied, some kola nuts, a pint of palm wine, and grilled maize in palm oil. After some incantations during which he invoked the spirits of dead relatives to come and witness the event, the family head took out a sharp knife and slid the neck of the cock in a single blow. He directed the blood that spurted out into the hole in front of him. Seven elderly members of the family were requested to spit into the hole. Spittle and blood were mixed into a concoction. It did not feel good to look at and Dion was afraid he might be asked to drink it. He had had to drink similar concoctions before. That was when he was a frail teenage boy, suffering from hepatitis. He was so ill and it was believed that he could be treated only by native medicines and native medicines meant such concoctions. He drank them and got well, but then he had not known nor seen how they came about. In the case he was witnessing, to drink a concoction of the fresh blood of a cock and the spittle of several old people would be quite a brave feat. He fervently prayed that he would not be asked to drink it. Fortunately, his prayers were listened to. The concoction was meant for smearing and not for drinking. Each of the seven people who had spat into the hole had to step forward to smear Dions chest with the concoction using their thumbs. As they took turns they repeated some parts of an incantation which built up to the following words:

> *It is with utmost humility*
> *And for the undying unity*
> *of this whittling family*
> *which death has visited so often*
> *and taken away all the able*
> *leaving behind only children*
> *and the disabled*
> *That I ...call on you all*
> *The spirits of our forefathers,*
> *fathers and of course mothers*
> *to share with us the mortals*
> *on this glorious day, kola nuts*
> *food , water and palm wine*
> *that one of your unmistakable*
> *children: Dion Ekpochaba*
> *has brought and placed before you*
> *because he recognizes that you*
> *the spirits of his ancestors have*
> *fanned and propped him to prominence*
> *and he is about to leave this land*
> *Of his ancestors and go to*
> *some faraway land*

9

in search of wisdom,
white man's wisdom
Which we think has overtaken ours
and taken control of everything
that belonged to us.
This wisdom will enable him
Cope with new realities,
realizations and responsibilities.
The road to this land
is riddled with much, much danger.
and many, many hurdles.
And his mission to this land
is to drink, as much as possible
from the white man's fountains.
Something which, any ordinary
person, who has grown up in his
own whims and ways would find
very, very difficult to achieve.
O ancestors! Our ancestors!
Your child: Dion Ekpochaba
wants you, yonder, in the spirit world
to be aware of this.
So, come, oh come, the undaunted spirits
that look after this family ,every day, every night.
Come with your potent blessings,
Blessings that will clear thorns, puddles and pits off
the paths, all the paths he will walk through.
Blessings that will enable him
live over there from success to success and in peace
and then get back to us in one blessed piece
to ensure the continuity of this family
and assume the responsibilities that await him.
For we believe that as a cocoyam rots away
It surely leaves behind a nodule to ensure
continuity.

Every one of the elderly took a turn in the smearing exercise and by the time they had finished, Dion's entire chest, broad as it was, was smeared with the concoction. He was advised not to have a bath for two days.

At the end of the ritual, the head of the family brought out an amulet from the depth of an elongated calabash saying: "this Dion, stands for the spirit of your late father and all those of all his brothers and sisters who had gone before and after him and also the spirits of his parents, your grandparents. They all live in the world on the other side. This amulet should always remind you, wherever you go that they, the dead are always with you in spirit and they wish you well. Give the amulet the respect it is due. It will please the ancestors to know that modern science has done nothing to tarnish your faith in the beliefs of your people and their ancestors. You must not desecrate it. You must wear it with reverence, around your neck, whenever and wherever you feel threatened."

The amulet was then handed over to Dion and he solemnly swore to jealously keep it, protect it and also use it appropriately.

e had been in England for quite a bit and he had not had any cause to have recourse to his amulet. But on that day that he hit his left foot on the doorstop, he felt, something was wrong somewhere. Evil was lurking somewhere, ready to rear its ugly head and pounce on any unfortunate bystander. He had to make sure he was not that unfortunate bystander. He held his amulet confidently, meditated awhile and put it round his neck. Then he wore a jacket over his shirt. The time was exactly half past two when he stepped out of his Tocil flat forty residence to embrace the aggressiveness of the intense sunshine. Quite intense, for an autumn afternoon. Apparently, even the British seasons were becoming as unpredictable as their weather. Dion wandered leisurely to the Westwood part of the campus, admiring especially the sports complex near Arden house, with its special athletics facilities. He wondered how a university could have such a beautiful and up-to-date sports complex and his entire country could not boast just one. In spite of that, like England, his country had qualified for the nineteen-ninety soccer event that was going to take place in Italy. Then he walked down through the footpath to the Advanced Technology Centre and then back to the main road leading to Gibbet Hill. Before walking up to Gibbet Hill, he stopped at Cryfield village, a student residential area that had been built to sip in the pleasure of contact with rural beauty – serene air, serene structures, serene ambiance and serene scenery. He then walked on to Gibbet Hill, where the departments of Mathematics and Biological sciences operated. The quietude was quite complete as there were no students hustling in and out of lecture theatres. The peace of the place made him to continue to wander around it. As he did so, a thought sailed through and anchored in his mind. Someone had told him that Gibbet Hill had been the hanging place of many a hardcore criminal. It should therefore be a place haunted by the spirits of all the hardened criminals who had been hanged there. The thought took his mind back home where it was believed that the buildings housing the Language Centre, where he worked used to be the National House of Assembly and most of those who had debated government bills in the House had died. Every night, their spirits returned there to carry on with the work they had been doing during their lifetime. The guards who worked night shift had told stories of people shouting in the buildings at night and banging the tables. They had heard distinct voices debating the laws of the new republic and the speaker calling for order. There was also the story of a family that had rented a villa. Each morning, when they got up they found the remains of food in the living room. And so one day, the family decided to stay up late into the night to find out what had been happening. They had all gathered in one of the bedrooms in wait. All the lights had been switched off. At exactly one o'clock in the morning, they started to hear movements in the living room. People wearing white clothes, getting in and taking their seats. Soon after, there was noise like food being dished, and then there was eating, people leaking their fingers noisily. The people were distinctly seen in their white clothes. Then suddenly, the head of the family stretched his hand onto the switch that lit the living room and pressed it on. The lights came on but all the white clothing disappeared. However, there was food left on the table. The family couldn't wait for the day to break completely. As soon as it was half past five, their father went and hired a truck and the family moved out in great haste.

Dion had grown up learning about stories of ghosts. His people strongly believe that no-one from their tribe especially those who die young do stay in their graves. They usually rose after burial to continue the rest of their life elsewhere. But before they left for their new homes, they hovered around to collect a few things. People have testified having met such ghosts and even exchanged words with them. Some who were said to be wicked had been caught and burned in public. Unfortunately, Dion had never been part of the public that witnessed such burning. So the concept had remained a mystery to him.

Here he was in another country and he had become aware of the possible crippling mystery that reigned around the grounds he was treading on. He suddenly felt unsafe, and had to stop nosing around there. He quickly made a U-turn and walked down again to the main campus. On his way, he found a conserved woodland – Tocil woodland. He walked into it hoping to find at least a viper or a black mamba, which would remind him of home. But nothing of that sort was in sight, not even their own kind of snakes – if there were any. He longed to see one because a snake by its very nature symbolizes nobility. It is harmful but never harms for the sake of harming. The woodland was apparently void of wildlife, but for a miserable squirrel here and another there.

Dion really felt disappointed about the concept of forest in England. They did not grow out thick, green and full of wildlife like they were in his country. In his disappointment, he walked away from the woodland and found himself face to face with a lake. He had never known that anything like that existed on the campus. Ever since he got there most of his business had been with the hostel, classroom, library, restaurant, bank and the supermarket. It was therefore a great pleasure for him to find himself at the banks of the lake – humbly lying on part of the lowland that separated Gibbet Hill from the main campus. It was also an honour to be in the presence of calm, symbolized by the piece of art that was the lake. It earnestly kept within its bounds in perfect humility, even though its warmth of heart irresistibly attracted both friend and foe. He soon found himself a seat on the west bank of the lake. He sat and watched exuberant moorhens swimming trustingly in the water, which provoked the creeping in of a nostalgic feeling. The good old days when he used to swim compulsively in the lake Barombi, with its very refreshing water trapped in a time-honoured

15

crater. He also thought about the Awing lake and then the Nyos. What a thought to jump in at that time, when he was looking forward to having a pleasant time at the shores of a lake. To remember Lake Nyos was to remember death. People were still wondering whose fault it was. The innocuous water, created by God for salutary purposes must not stand accused. At that point, Dion's eyes went misty and he was soon blinded by tears. He went into a momentary trance. When he returned to himself, he felt some strange freshness, all over his body and soul. It was strange, and refreshing at the same time. He got up and walked back calmly to his hall of residence, very satisfied that he had had a very refreshing day. And besides, he had found a source of comfort and inspiration – the lake, which he hoped to turn to from time to time.

Chapter Four

Back in his room, Dion took off his jacket, intending to have a nap before facing up to the demands of the evening. As he was unbuttoning his shirt he realized that the thing that hung on the string around his neck was gone. It was no longer there, the amulet. He held the string that held it and took it off his neck and half consciously asked "where's the amulet that you were holding? Tell me before I harm you. The ecstasy that had radiated from his eyes was suddenly replaced by terror and agony. Like a bulldog struck by rabies, he rushed out of the room, forgetting even to close the door. He ran back to all the paths through which he had just walked. He ran along them, peering at every corner, in case his eyes fell on his cherished amulet. After he had combed the paths of Tocil, Westwood, Cryfield and Gibbet Hill to no avail, he rushed down to the lake. Still he could not see any sign of his lost object. He started shouting in spite of himself " nchung, aah nchung, woh yie eh?" – his native language for "amulet, amulet, where can you possibly be now?" He waited for an answer but he got none. He made other desperate appeals to the amulet but still there was no response. He then realized that as long as he was still in the United Kingdom, he would get no answer, till thy kingdom come. He could not help breaking down in tears: "O look at me Ekpochaba, what carelessness, what misfortune, for me to lose my own soul. How could I have

17

done this to myself? O it's impossible, impossible, impossible."

As he rummaged around the lake weeping in despair, a tall strong-looking English man who was rambling around the lake with his dog noticed him. He was on the mature side of his sixties, although he still walked with sufficient firmness and gait. He was attracted by Dion's behaviour and so decided to walk up to him, his dog faithfully trailing behind.

"Are you all right?" he asked firmly.

"Me? No, I'm not all right as you can notice," Dion replied.

"What's the matter? Maybe I can be of help or at least some of it. By the way, my name's Tom. Tom Jones, a retired military officer."

"I'm Dion, Dion Ekpochaba. A graduate student at the university. I'm a bit out of my mind right now because I've just run out of luck. I've lost something precious. In fact very precious to me."

"Your girlfriend or something?"

"Girlfriend! You must be joking. How can I consider a girlfriend precious?" Dion asked.

"Depends on how you regard friendship. I thought you had come rambling around the lake with your girlfriend and she had gone missing. Anyway, what might this precious thing be then?" Tom Jones inquired.

" Eh m, ehmmm, no use mentioning it to you. You know nothing about it and you won't understand anything if I start explaining. It's something very personal and traditional too. I don't know how to talk about it to an Englishman," Dion said disappointedly.

"Come on, say something. If you know something say it and it would be left for the person to whom you say it to understand or misunderstand you."

"That's the point. I don't want to be misunderstood."

"Not by me anyway," said Tom Jones. I know quite a bit about your people and their traditions."

"My people! Who are my people?" Dion asked.

"Your African people. I've lived and worked there."

"Well, it depends on where in Africa. Africa isn't a country, it's a continent. A vast one, at that. You might have lived and worked in Egypt, Morocco, Botswana and Burkina Faso, and that doesn't bring you anywhere close to a resumé of Africa."

"To be specific young man, I worked in the highlands of Cameroon. I led the regiment that stayed at the old fort in Bamenda."

"Did I hear you say Cameroon?"

"Yes, I said Cameroon and I worked in Bamenda."

"Can the world be this small?" Dion wondered aloud. "Imagine me in a sea of white people, with a sprinkle of blacks here and there, never hoping any of the whites had set foot in Africa, talk less of Cameroon, my dear country. And here am I standing face to face with a white man who had defended the interest of his people

19

from the brutality of another European country on the soil of my country. I had thought that all the ashes of colonization had been blown into the great oceans. Now, it stares at me in flesh and in blood, in the person of a certainTom Jones."

Nevertheless, a ray of hope swept through the mind of Dion Ekpochaba as the Englishman spoke so intelligibly about his country. Since his arrival in England, he had not met any Englishman on the streets, nor anywhere in the City who knew, where the hell, the country, Cameroon was located on the world map. Many of them could only guess that Cameroon was somewhere in black Africa because of his accent and blackness of skin. It was therefore a great surprise for him to meet Tom Jones. He decided he would explain his problem to him. He might not give answers to his problems but he could suggest ideas which might lead him to find answers.

"Sir," Dion began.

"Call me Tom, please," Tom said .

Dion paused. He thought that it was out of place. He found the culture rather strange. How would he start calling an elderly person like Mister Tom Jones by his first name. A man on whose neck the title Papa should be hung. Papa Tom should be a most suitable appellation for him. Dion's teachers in the university had also insisted on the first name issue and it was really an issue amongst some of them, African students. They had been used to calling people by their titles, especially those who had become chiefs, doctors and professors. Recently the trend was moving to include the professions people practice. Economists were insisting on being called Economist Bojoko for example, Architect Njongolo, Lawyer Peeters, Engineer Martins etc. And then a man who should have insisted on being called Veteran Tom Jones was asking to be called, simply Tom. Dion was however getting used to it. As they say, in Rome do as the Romans.

"OK Tom, you see, I've just lost an amulet. It's not a piece of jewellery, like your dictionaries might say. Rather, it's a piece of leather strewn into a bloat. In it are some dried up forest plants and other traditional paraphernalia. This object represents the presence of my ancestors around me. I reckon you understand what that means. It has a string attached to it allowing it to be put around the neck. I had gone out of my flat having it around my neck but it just disappeared from my neck. I cannot even conjecture how it happened but it disappeared just like that. I only discovered, that was the case when I had returned to my room after a walk around. I'm terribly afraid of the wrath of my family, both the living and the dead, when they get to know that the amulet they had given me, and which I had promised them, I would keep jealously, has disappeared. I may have the luxury of explaining the misfortune to the living in my family and they may understand and forgive my carelessness, but how about the dead? How do I contact them in order to explain? You see the predicament, sir, sorry Tom, in which I have thrown myself?" Dion said remorsefully.

"I do understand your plight Dion, but the amulet to which you and your family are so attached is in the depth of that lake. I had thrown it there roughly five minutes before you came, desperately looking for it."

Immediately, Dions eyes turned deep red and he could not help raising his voice:

"You did what? You did what to my amulet? How could you have been so ...And for God's sake, how did you come by it?"

In spite of Tom's knowledge of the people of Cameroon and their values, he was not amused by the sudden outrage of, and the insults from the young man. He, however, kept his cool and tried to explain:

"I'm awfully sorry, young man. I have inadvertently hurt you. If I were still resident in your country I would have kept the amulet as soon as I saw it, knowing how your people value things like that. But finding a bloated form of leather here in the U.K did not quite ring a bell. I did not even have the slightest inkling that the object could be useful property for someone. So when I found it, all I could do was throw it away. It was Jim, my dog that called my attention to it. I noticed him playing with it and scratching the leather, and I picked it up, examined it halfheartedly and then flung it into space. It flew upwards and then landed in the middle of the lake. I thought it might float but instead it sank as soon as it landed in the water."

As Dion listened, he felt like strangling the old man. He thought he could even challenge him to a man-to-man combat in order to thoroughly teach him a lesson. A bitter lesson that objects, when found, should not be toyed with and thrown away with levity. He looked at the old man's face and a creeping thought came to him about his grandfather and then his father, both of whom had died quite some years ago. It would be an abomination back home if he showed his strength against an old man, even to unleash his anger. Immediately, he became aware of the harsh words that he had just unleashed on the old man. He thought of offering an apology but he changed his mind. Dion thought for a while about the ongoing events and recognized that all though many things were at stake, he did not have to show irreverence against old age. He had the feeling that he might have been rude to the old man because he himself had asked him to simply call him Tom, Tom, as if they were age-mates or playmates, ignoring the well known fact that familiarity breeds contempt. Dion quickly made up his mind to be calm and responded much less reproachfully to the situation.

"Naturally Sir, I beg your pardon, Tom, the amulet had to sink. It had become impotent, having been desecrated, in fact raped by none other creature than a dog. There was no way the amulet could again float."

Dion turned to face the lake, knocking off his shoes. Instantly, Tom Jones knew what he was up to. His experience in the army had taught him so much about the irrational behaviour of young people. Because of that, they had usually been the ones to be sent on suicide missions and they always agreed to go without second thoughts. He thought of how, some sinister organizations would recruit and manipulate them to carry out high risk operations. They never had time to regret their actions.

"Wait a minute," Tom shouted as he watched him go towards the lake.

Dion hesitated and then stood to hear what the old man was going to say.

"I know what you're going to do. You want to plunge into the lake. That would be putting your life at risk. It's true your eh amulet is of great value to you but your life has immeasurable value and you can't afford to lose it now. Come back to your senses and consider the pain your death would cause your people back home. Reconsider the action you're about to take. It's very risky young man." Tom advised.

"There's no turning back, Tom," Dion said stubbornly. "The decision I've taken is final. I'll either execute it or I die."

Tom Jones thought for a moment, and was convinced that no amount of pleading would restrain the young man from executing his plans, so he resorted to threats.

"Now, turn and look at me awhile," he said softly to Dion.

Dion obeyed and he said to him, "you see this dog. It can be as wild as a wolf if I let it loose. I suppose you'd prefer a more subtle death than be torn apart by a hungry and angry dog. It has missed its lunch because we have been out here and now it is very hungry. So if I make a signal to him this minute, you'll be turned into minute pieces of meat and clean bones. If you don't want that to happen to you, drop the idea that is lingering on your mind."

Dion gave a quick glance at the fierce-looking Jim and understood that Tom Jones meant business. He then looked at the dog more closely and hated it for being a threat to his plans and hated it even more for raping his amulet. It was never supposed to be smelt by a dog, let alone using its paws on it. And then if he made any mistakes himself, he would become lunch and dinner for the dog.

"Tom please," he pleaded meekly, "give me a chance to do what I want to do. It is not even for me but for others. I know what I'm saying better than anyone else around me. I do understand my intentions better. If I don't retrieve the amulet from the depth of this lake, a great calamity would descend on this area and there would be misery all over the place."

"Misery or no misery, I can't allow you to drown before my eyes. Nothing can convince me that you'll plunge into this lake and come out alive. I know it better than you do and I wonder you haven't read the warning at the entrance against any attempts to swim or do boating in it. I guess you take warning notices seriously."

"I had read it but I'm a child of the coast. A day after I was born I was thrown in water to test my swimming instincts and I passed the test. I can swim in both rivers and seas, Tom. I can swear that I'm a very good swimmer. I can go down the depth of the lake and spend at least thirty minutes looking for the amulet and come out successfully. As I had said before, if you don't let me do it, calamity and misery will hang over this area for a very long time. This beautiful campus will have all the beautiful people resident in it swept off at one fell swoop. As a matter of fact, it won't be just the campus but also the entire population of Coventry City, Leamington Spa, Kenilworth and Warwickshire. Imagine such a calamity likely to befall your country anytime from now, and I'm here willing to offer myself to prevent it and you are there doing everything to prevent me. Please, Tom give me the opportunity to save humanity one grim picture too many. Cooperate with me so that families all over the world are spared long periods of mourning."

"Are you all right upstairs?" Tom asked baffled.

"Why not? If I'm all right downstairs, what prevents me from being the same upstairs."

"Upstairs and downstairs are opposites and one is likely to be okay one way and not okay the other. As things are, I still believe you are not okay upstairs."

"I don't expect you to believe in what I say, but all I request is that you let me help avert a disaster before time runs out." Dion said, his voice sounding urgent.

"Wait a minute Dion, what makes you believe so firmly that the sinking of your amulet down the lake will result in this crazy picture you have painted." Tom Jones asked with so much interest.

"It's unfortunate that you take me for a madman, but remember that sometimes wisdom comes from foolishness and madness. Was

Galileo not thought to be pregnant with madness when he first intimated that planet earth was not flat as widely accepted, but spherical? If you insist on not taking me seriously, within hours, this lake will start, simmering and then go on to boiling."

"Boiling. Did you say boiling?" asked Tom.

"Yes, I said boiling and the lake will actually start boiling," Dion said with much conviction. " When it comes to invisible forces causing havoc, call it black magic if you like, there's nothing like mercy. It isn't quite half a decade yet when such forces gripped a part of my country. A symbol of tradition, like the one you have thrown in that lake, was raped and thrown in a lake called Nyos, causing a stir in the entire region. The gods of the lake got so angry that eight hours after the incident, the water started boiling and emitting a strange gas that engulfed the surrounding areas, consuming life out of anything that had it. Some people were lucky not to have lost their heads completely. They found respite in palm oil and they drank it and survived. The gas caused burns and palm oil was also used to treat the burns of those who survived. Whole villages were crippled, bereft of their inhabitants, leaving only lifeless structures to bear the strictures of barrenness. Heaps after heaps of people , men, women and children of all ages lost their lives and they could not be given decent burials as there were no persons to do that for them. The government could only afford mass graves to get rid of the corpses. Tom, even as I tell you this story now, I still shudder, I have

27

never been witness to any event as gruesome as that. When it comes to being angry, the gods are unequalled. They are simply terrible."

"Are you sure of what you're talking about?"

"Once more Tom, I'm not mad. I'm as sure of what I'm saying as I'm my dear mother's first son."

"Well, Dion, when did this terrible thing happen?"

"I can remember the date very well, I'm not so good at keeping dates. Sometimes I forget the date of my own birth but as for the date of the catastrophe, I shall never ever forget. It happened on 21st August 1986".

"And you say, all the people of the surrounding villages were robbed of their lives."

"Yes, almost all the people including, their cattle and other animals both domestic and wild and even insects and plants. I'm very surprised Tom that this information is new to you, even though when the catastrophe occurred, Nyos became the journalists' salt pond. Many countries raced to Cameroon in search of news on Nyos and also to provide relief aid. This Great Britain of yours was one of the countries that sent assistance," said Dion.

"It sure did, it sent aid, this Great Britain of ours. It's not for nothing that it's great. I remember I got some vague reports about some sinister gas in some remote part of Africa and that didn't quite catch my attention, especially because events like that have become common currency. It's only now that I'm getting some meaning out of it. The severity of the event is beginning to dawn on me only now. What did you say were the villages affected?"

"Subum, Fang, Cam Nyos and eh ..er…"

"Did you say Fang?"

"Yes I did"

"Do you mean everyone in Fang died?"

"Yes, especially because no one there thought of the palm oil therapy. However, those whom fate had carted away from the village on that fateful day may still be alive but they were only a handful."

"Damn it!" exclaimed Tom Jones. What a pity! I had helped rehabilitate the people of Fang after the Second World War. They had been devastated by the war and like the Jews the people of Fang had been scattered all over the country, homeless. One of my assignments after the war was to rehabilitate them. I was then a young exuberant soldier, serving in the British colonial army. It was the first time in my life to feel really close to other human beings that did not belong to my race. They were a vulnerable lot and it had to take a lot of assuring to bring back their humanity. And I succeeded very well. The people looked on me as the new founder of their tribe and I made many friends among them, one of whom was the chief. He was a very dynamic and open-minded person, who was very people-centred. When I left Cameron, I was very positive I had left the Fang people in very good hands because I trusted the chief. We had been in touch with each other for a couple of years but owing to the exigencies of life, we lost touch and it's a shame that I'm getting to know about the fatal fate of the people only now. It is hard to believe that all those friendly people and their offspring have died so dismally en masse. What a shame!"

As the Englishman spoke, he started shivering like someone suffering from an attack of high fever. Shortly after, he was lying sprawled on the ground. He appeared to have been seized by a fit. He was stretching out his limbs like a sheep about to give up the last breath. Jim, his dog seemed to have forgotten his hunger and stood whining desperately over his master. Dion was very shaken by the turn of events. He was too shocked to make any sense out of what was unfolding in front of him. At one moment an apparently strong-looking man was all threatening, and then the very next moment the same man was all crumbling and sprawling on the ground. He, however, set his mind working fast. He rushed to the nearest telephone booth and dialed 999.

ion Ekpochaba was not a neophyte in witnessing fits. As a form one pupil in a boarding school he had witnessed his most intimate friend succumb to violent fits during an early morning roll call ritual. The young man was patiently standing on his own row of form one pupils, waiting for his turn to answer present. But when his turn came, it became a struggle for him to voice out the word that had hung in his mind ever since the senior prefect, started calling the first names on the class list. He had shaped his mouth to say present but the voiceless 'P' got stuck between his lips. All that the senior prefect, his classmates, and some of the rows behind them could here was a protracted 'p...p...p' sound. Then the fits seized him violently and the shivering form of his friend could no longer hold itself upright. He watched him go down on all fours, a foaming substance coming out of his mouth. Everyone including Dion was scared. They all thought that death had paid them an early morning visit, looking for likely victims. The school was in an uproar. Pupils, including the senior prefect, were running in every imaginable direction. The patient, unconscious of what was happening was abandoned to himself and his fate. Fortunately, the Principals residence was in the premises of the school and the uproar had attracted him to the roll call ground. He found the patient lying sprawled on the ground and he found out that he had just had epileptic fits. The school nurse was

31

immediately brought in and the situation was taken care of. Nevertheless, the boy found it very hard to reintegrate in the school system. Other pupils became scared of him, looking on him as one who had been visited by death. He suddenly became an untouchable even to his intimate friend, Dion. The boy found it difficult to cope with the environment and so, one fine day, his parents came to collect him for treatment at home and since then he never returned. Dion, however, received a letter from him, a year later that he had been completely treated of the illness. As Dion matured, he was made to believe that epilepsy was an illness that was contracted only by accursed persons. The only means of contracting it was through witchcraft. A witch or wizard had to cast it on the victim like a spell. It had nothing to do with nature and so it could only be treated by sorcerers. After the experience of his classmate, Dion had witnessed other cases of people going into a fit. There was a case of a young man of about twenty who usually went into a fit whenever he was talking to a girl he was about to win. Everyone believed that he had been cursed never to have a girlfriend. In the case of Tom Jones, Dion refused to believe that it could be a case of epilepsy. "How would anyone cast a spell on a white man?" he wondered. He was therefore at a loss as to what might have caused the fits of his newest acquaintance, Mr. Tom Jones. Shortly after, an ambulance drove in, in response to the 999 call.

Strangely, soldiers, not ambulance workers were jumping out of the vehicle. He started wondering, what the hell soldiers had to do with a dying patient. It was a health issue, not a war one. It was then it struck him that they might have replaced the ambulance workers who had been on a long drawn strike. The soldiers were possibly of the medical corps of the military. The country was lucky that the soldiers were there to replace ambulance staff. What if they had been deployed to some war front, where they belong? Strikes were an interesting feature of his host country. Such a phenomenon would never have existed in his own country, if they had even one fifth of the facilities that were provided workers in the United Kingdom. That was a place where even the jobless were paid a salary, not even at the end of the month but at the end of every week. It was a place where a room cleaner did his job with a smile on their face, an indication that they were not working on an hungry stomach. Yet they went on strike, and the strikes were persistent. Then it was the ambulance staff. Soon after, it would be transport workers, and so on. Yet they each lived in at least a flat with constant electricity and decent toilet facilities.

"Back at home," Dion Ekpochaba reflected, "endurance was the key word. One day, the end of the tunnel would be reached. While waiting for this day, the jobless in their millions hang on the 'jobful' and the misery of life goes on track, deep into the tunnel, hoping the end would come soon. Very few think of a strike. How can one strike when they thrive on hope?"

The soldiers handled the situation skillfully and promptly Tom Jones was driven off to one of the hospitals in the city. The ambulance staff could not have done better. Dion later found out that it was Walsgrave Hospital.

These events had temporarily taken Dion's mind away from his raped amulet. Many people had been around him pestering him with questions about what had happened and he lost count of the number of times he had repeated himself. He was fagged out by the time he opened his room and walked in. He slumped on his bed and yearned for sleep. But when his right palm touched his neck, he had a feeling that something had been forgotten. Then he remembered the amulet. It was already quite dark outside, but stealthily he walked back to the shores of the lake, his heart hitting hard against his chest for fear that anytime, the water would start boiling. He dipped his right hand into the water expecting it would have started getting warm, but instead it was freezing cold. He was surprised but he still felt like rescuing the amulet. He looked at the blank layer of still water as it lay in the darkness and thought it was a wise idea not to succumb to his will. It was obviously going to be a futile attempt to try to rescue the amulet at that time. He examined himself and felt ashamed. Ashamed, because the threatening misadventure was his making – his carelessness. He did not bother so much about his own fate, but that of others – all the beautiful people around him. The exuberant young people on campus who led their lives in the way that anyone who cared to observe would think that the future belonged to them, the boisterous young people who played hard and equally worked hard. By the following morning, the campus would be a ghost one, the city itself and the neighbouring towns and villages would all have gone, emptied of their living beings and not a soul would be there to tell the story of what had actually happened. It would be a field period for scientists and all to speculate, breaking new ground after new ground. They would swarm in from all the angles of mother earth, testing every testable thing and formulating hypothesis after hypothesis which they would nurture into theory after theory, just to satisfy their whims and caprices as the rest of the world would look on and listen to them, flabbergasted. The true theory would be lying buried in him, Dion Ekpochaba. He felt like leaving a note behind. It would clarify the entire world, letting them not to wonder at what happened. But he thought that no-one would take his note seriously. A scientific world was too scientific to give credence to primitive beliefs, especially when such beliefs come from a not-so-scientific Africa.

Dion gave up everything for lost and returned to his room, his heart still throbbing. He was thoroughly tired and hungry but he thought it was a waste to eat anything. He lay down on his bed prepared to die, feeling sorry for those who generated the laughter that spilled over, from the adjoining rooms. They would be surprised by the drama of death. That was the advantage he had over them or it could be they who had an advantage over him. His thoughts pulled him to

35

all the places he had been to and he met all the
people he had met before in the course of his
short life. He fell asleep, in spite of, himself and
descended into a very deep slumber.

he following morning, when he opened his eyes, his room had been invaded by the light of dawn. He remembered the events of the previous day and then he thought for a while and was not quite sure as to what side of the world he belonged to. He rubbed his eyes, opened them wider and recognized that nothing had changed. His room was still the same with books and scraps of paper scattered on the floor, on the table, chairs and even on the bed. He could not believe it. He wondered at what might have prevented him from descending yet. Without considering that he ought to do his toilet first thing in the morning, he got out of his room and walked down the corridor into the staircase and out of the flat. He ran to the lake and found its water cold and peaceful. He dipped his fingers into it, took them out quickly and turned towards his flat. It was already more than fourteen hours since his amulet got drowned in the lake and nothing had happened.

"Maybe," thought Dion Ekpochaba, " the gods have gone to sleep."

Dion made up his mind to go to Walsgrave hospital to visit Mr Tom Jones. He had decided to forego his classes for the entire day. He took the number nine bus to the hospital. He discovered that Tom had already been discharged from the hospital and he had returned to his home. He requested for his address, giving reasons why he wanted it. The hospital authorities were quite understanding and they

37

gave him. He found Tom's home at number 48 Chancellor close, Cannon Park. It was only about twenty minutes walk from the university. When he ran the doorbell and the door opened, he was very surprised that it was Tom himself who met him at the door and asked him in. His faithful Jim was on his heels, wagging its tail.

"Di..on, am I right?," asked Tom Jones.

"You're quite right" answered Dion.

"Nice to see you. I knew you would come. Have a seat."

"How did you know I would come, Tom?"

"I'm very familiar with the hospitable attitude of your people. Don't forget I've lived with them."

"I see. Thank you for the compliment and for receiving me," Dion said warmly.

"How did you find yourself here. I'm sure we didn't exchange addresses, did we?" Tom asked.

"No, we didn't, but my people say that a dog that can make use of its nose, never loses its way. Same applies to a man that can make use of his mouth," said Dion touching his mouth.

"That's clever Dion. So whom did you ask from?"

"When I got up today, I discovered myself alive and the rest of Coventry too. I then thought about you and what had happened to you, so I went directly to the hospital, where I was informed you had gone back home. Anxious to see you, I asked for your home address from the hospital authorities."

"Very kind of you, Dion, anything I can do for you, young man?" Tom inquired."

"Anything you can do for me? But you were seriously ill yesterday, almost at a break neck situation, so for no other reason, I should come and see you and find out how you are doing. It embarrasses me when you ask if you can do anything for me. I didn't come to your house, so that you do something for me. I came because I care."

"Thank you very much. Well, Dion, it was nothing serious, it happened to have been one of those bouts of fits that overcome me from time to time. All I needed was a few doses of phenytoin and a lot of rest to feel all right again. It was the first time the fits had taken hold of me in the open, like that. I better get you some coffee," he said disappearing into his kitchen.

Dion had become very used to the offer of coffee or tea. English people felt very honoured and happy offering their guest either of these, and they did it in very tiny teacups. Back home, guests were offered a bottle of cold beer and sometimes food, when it was available. Over here, you didn't have to expect food when you had not been invited for it. While waiting for his cup of coffee, Dion leaned back on the armchair and tried to understand a few things around him. Here was a man who was on the brink of death the previous day telling him, it was nothing serious. He was an elderly man whom he had thought should be living in a home with a large family, with family members tumbling over one another to take care of him. But strangely enough, he seemed to have been struggling with existence all by himself. He had just been rescued from the fangs of death, yet his house was empty of people who had come to sympathise with him and assure him of their constant support. If it was back home, the news of his illness would have gone far and wide and Tom Jones would have had an entire village in his house, a mark of solidarity and concern for human life. It was however true that his living space was quite small. The living room where he was sitting, was only about twelve square metres. In it were two armchairs and a sofa. There was a small bookshelf to the left of the sofa, a staircase to the right and directly behind it was the doorway into the kitchen. There was, at least a bedroom upstairs. There was adequate comfort in the house but it lacked space. Back home, houses were not necessarily built with much finesse but there was much space. He knew of a home whose living room was half a football field. The dining table could comfortably sit thirty people at a time. Apparently such small space for homes was a function of their climatic conditions. The bigger the space, the more costly the heating, especially in Winter.

As the thoughts spun around his mind, the English man returned with two cups of hot coffee.

"Well, Dion, I presume you had no classes at the university today," Tom said, handing him his cup of coffee.

"I had classes Tom, but I decided to sacrifice them in order to know what was going on with you. I can always make up, later."

"Well, here I am, hale and hearty, don't you think?"

"Yes, but you were as good as dead yesterday. What crossed my mind was that you had had a massive heart attack."

"Heart attack! I wouldn't have been here talking to you now. As a matter of fact, it was an epileptic fit. A few years after my retirement from the army, I started suffering from epilepsy. Occasionally, the fits overcome me and yesterday was one of those unfortunate days. I guess you were scared stiff. It is one of those illnesses that take away one's consciousness. It is very humiliating, you know.

"Sure it is, and as you had said earlier, I was very scared. I even thought that it was the effect of my raped amulet, since yours were the last human hands that touched it. Later, I thought that it was the story about Lake Nyos in my country that had been instrumental in inducing the fits. I thought of all kinds of things."

"It was a mere coincidence that the fits came at the time they came. The stories, no matter how shocking, shouldn't have induced a fit. And you too Dion, have recovered your senses."

"I don't think I ever lost them Tom," said Dion calmly.

"But you were all nagging yesterday about wishing to save lives by first losing yours. What madness."

"And I meant it."

"Meant what? Come on, don't start it again. Don't you realize the whole fuss has turned out to be a whole farce, or have you retrieved the amulet from the bowels of the lake?"

"No, Tom." Dion said shaking his head from side to side.

"If the amulet is still where I had thrown it, why is nothing happening?"

"Maybe the gods, the gods of my ancestors have gone lame under a foreign sky."

"It could also be that the lakes of England have a magic wand against evil," said Tom Jones teasingly.

Dion thought of what to say but nothing worth saying could cross his mind. So he just sat on the armchair looking at the tiny teacup he had kept on the side stool. He had emptied the cup in one gulp. As for Tom, his cup was still half full and he was sipping the coffee gradually, not bothering whether Dion's cup was empty or not. His dog, Jim was lying at his feet and he was stroking his head. Later, Tom decided to break the silence.

"Dion, are your people still peace loving, warm and inordinately optimistic? I was really tongue-tied at the fact that such a large group of people who didn't share a single mother tongue and had a great many differences in culture could stay together under a single umbrella called, Cameroon. What was even more striking was the fact that some of those tribes that were brought up by us, the British, bundled themselves together to join people who had been brought up by frogs, the French. What a leap in the dark? It sure demonstrated some stupidity or was it being inordinately optimistic?"

"It would be insulting, Tom to think that my people were stupid. Would it be stupid for children born of the same mother but brought up in different homes to say they belong to the same family, and would want to live together as a family? I think my people are inordinately optimistic. They thought they would take advantage of both the British experience and the French experience. As you have me studying in one of your best universities here in Britain, so do the French have my French-speaking brother studying in La Sorbonne. By the time we return home, we shall surely be very useful to our country. As for the peace back home, it is predicated on the fact that the Cameroonian is never hungry, and by God's grace can never be hungry. There's peace where there's no hunger. Another factor that makes us proud of ourselves is that in spite of our numerous mother tongues, everybody else depends on everybody else. And if everybody else depends on everybody else, there can't be absolute suffering nor absolute poverty, for never will all of us be poor all the time. So you see my people remain inordinately optimistic as you have observed." Dion said proudly.

"Good for them," Tom commented.

Dion shifted his hand a little and inadvertently knocked down his teacup, it fell but did not break. He picked it up and placed it where it had been. Then Tom asked if he would like more coffee. Of course he wanted more and Tom went to the kitchen again and came out with two cups of coffee. After a sip, Dion inquired:

"Now Tom, what about madam?"

"Madam? What do you mean? Asked Tom puzzled.

"I mean your wife." Dion said confidently.

"Ah, my wife! Wait a minute, I'll show you where she is."

Dion was surprised. How could his wife have been at home and they had been sitting there for near to an hour without her coming out to say hello. Was she ill or something? But he would have told him. Tom got up briskly and asked Dion to follow him. When he got to the door, he opened it gently as if he didn't want to disturb anyone. He showed Dion in and then pointed to a micro-computer and said calmly, " there, dear is my pretty little wife."

"But I can't see anyone." Dion complained.

"What have you seen, then?" asked Tom

"A micro-computer" said Dion, getting confused.

"That's her then. Lovely, intelligent and tolerant."

"You mean, you mean this computer is your wife?" Dion asked, very confused.

"Sure I mean it. Of what use is a wife to an old man like me?"

"Keeps him company at least."

"And precisely, that's what she does for me. Her name is Lisa. Lisa Amstrad." Tom said smiling.

Dion had no coffee in his mouth, so he swallowed saliva and returned to his seat. He said to himself that he had always thought wrongly that by the age of sixty, anyone would have known all that needed to be known on earth and so it was useless living beyond that age. But it appears knowledge about this earth was endless. He had never known that a man could take a computer for a wedded wife, just then he had learnt it. And the other day, he learnt that a man could have another man for wife. Ever since he got to the university he had heard so much about the gay society and decided to make an appearance at one of their meetings. It was then he got this new knowledge of men intimately linked to men and women intimately linked to women. He actually was caressed and kissed by another man. How awkward? But it was so normal and pleasurable to the members of the club. Dion had been regretting why he ever went to that club meeting but as they say, experience is the best teacher. During his early days on campus, he had been shocked when he visited a friend of his, an African brother, in one of the campus flats. He observed that all his flat mates were young women. He shared the same bathroom with them, the same toilets and of course same kitchen. He asked him how he felt living in the midst of women? He said he felt good, as long as the women didn't complain. Dion had wondered whether that was part of the culture but that case was an isolated one, so something might have gone wrong. Even more so because it was bastardly that the university authorities should have deliberately made such arrangements. It turned out that the name *Jean* French for *John* had been mistaken for the female name *Jean*. Also, there was the summer period when almost every white-skinned girl on campus went around half-naked. Dion found it very hard to manage the situation. There had been a good number of rape cases on campus that didn't seem like rape but because the law and the police were on the side of women the young men were incriminated. Dion would not like to be in their shoes, so he managed to buy a return ticket for his girlfriend who visited him that summer. The things he was going through were building him up but he felt very sorry for the old man, who was living with an illness as unpredictable as epilepsy and did not have the company of anyone but a dog.

hen Dion looked at his watch, he had spent two hours with Tom Jones. He told him he was returning to the campus. The old man thanked him for the visit and asked him to stop by, anytime he felt like. Then he remembered that Dion had not said anything about the survivors of the Lake Nyos incident. "Tell me," he said, "didn't anyone survive that disaster at Nyos?"

"Of course there were survivors. Many people intuitively drank palm oil as soon as they had that feeling of strangeness in them. Some were lucky that they had travelled out of home and were spared the brutal death."

"So what has happened to them?"

"Some of the assistance that came from friendly countries was channeled to them, although the bulk was plundered by government officials."

"Government officials! Are they not paid for the job they do?"

"Why not? Who on this earth can be an employee without pay? It is simply that none of them seems satisfied with their salary. So the least opportunity to embezzle is quickly taken advantage of."

"Not of victims of a terrible disaster like the one of Nyos."

"Who cares? Most people think that the misfortune of one person is the source of fortune for another. Even medication for the victims was swindled. Quite a number of people fed fat on the backs of the victims. All I can tell you is that many of them are very frustrated."

"I'm very sorry to hear that Dion but I thought there were safeguards to prevent such corrupt practices from happening."

"The safeguards may be there but they are overwhelmed by nepotism."

"I do understand you Dion. Once again, thank you for coming."

Just then Dion thought of something:

"Wait a minute Tom, this epilepsy of yours, isn't it curable here? Can't it be completely stopped from attacking you?"

"I doubt it, at least mine hasn't been cured permanently. All that the drugs I take do, is to reduce the intensity of the fits and also the frequency."

"You see Tom, there're traditional doctors, whom your people erroneously called witchdoctors, in my country who treat this epilepsy for good. The illness is still taboo there. No-one has the courage to be close to anyone who is epileptic. The belief that it is caused through the practice of witchcraft is still very strong back there. However, people have had treatment and they have never had the fits again. Apart from the rituals that the traditional doctors perform, they also use the sap which comes out of the trunk of a tree in one of our forests called 'ebangha'. The tree is found in only one forest, Korup. People come from all over the country to collect the sap of "ebangha." It is used for the treatment of several other illnesses.

"Korup!" that sounds familiar. I think the Prince of Wales is very interested in the forest. So, it has the famous healing plant?"

"Yes Tom"

"And what are you suggesting?"

"That you can go out to my country to have permanent treatment for your epilepsy."

"Are you sure I'll be treated?"

"There's no harm in trial, make a try and we shall see how it turns out. Besides, it will give you an opportunity to go back to Cameroon and appreciate how far it has gone after you had left it, for your own country."

"All right, Dion, I'll give it a thought, a very serious thought."

As Dion walked back to the campus, he was very certain about one thing; his safety in England no longer depended upon his cherished amulet. It had been raped and then buried at the bottom of an alien lake. It was gone for good and the luck in the matter was that it did not cause any harm – no single life was lost, nor any physical structure destroyed. His preoccupation was how he would tell his people about its loss. Or perhaps they already knew what had happened. He had much thinking to do to make his people believe some of the stories he would tell them. He wondered how he, a man, could be approached by another man, who wanted to use him as a woman. In his early days on the campus, a friend had taken him to a club meeting. During the meeting, the discussions were centred around discrimination and gay rights. He wondered who the hell were called gays. He looked around the room and he was the only black person. The others were handsome young men and stunningly beautiful young ladies. What was peculiar was the fact that they sat in pairs during the meeting and the pairs were *bone to bone* and *flesh to flesh,* instead of *bone to flesh* as usual. The friend who had taken him to the meeting made many attempts to caress him but each time he avoided his itchy fingers. Dion reflected on the word gay which he had always thought was positive and a very high frequency word which meant happy and full of fun. He wondered how much fun the young people around him were deriving from caressing their partners of the same sex. He found the whole thing very disgusting and felt very embarrassed to be in their midst. As soon as the meeting was over, he extricated himself from his friend and rushed to his room. He picked up his dictionary and looked up the word gay and behold the first definition was homosexual. So it was a homosexual club meeting he had been to? He was even more embarrassed. He blamed the situation on his language limitation, but he wondered when the word gay had evolved to assume its present status. He felt strongly that the dictionaries back home needed constant updating. A week after the experience with gays, he received an African friend. He had approached him and told him he too was an African from the North. He asked Dion not to mind his white skin because they were both the same inside. Two days into the relationship, Dion's friend was visiting him in his room. After entertaining his friend with some orange juice and biscuits, they started listening to some soft Cameroonian music. Dion's friend was so carried away with the rhythm that he jumped on him and before he could realise it he was being kissed all over the place and moans of *I love you, I love you Di.i..on* were spilling out of his desperate and shivering lips. It did not sound right in Dion's ears, considering that those words were coming out of masculine lips. Thanks to the gay meeting he had earlier attended, he quickly understood what was going on. It took a lot of tack to get him off Dion and more tact to get him out of the room. Dion had known that such practice was not unlawful in his host country and raising any alarm might have called for much misinterpretation. Then his mind went back to the man from whose home he had stepped out, not quite long ago. If he had not seen for himself, nothing would have convinced him that Tom Jones was living in a bare home. Not bare of property anyway, but bare of humans, apart from himself. He called a micro-computer his wife. Could it be possible that he had been married to a real woman? He had not said anything about his children. He might not have had any. That should explain why his intimacy to Jim was so faithful. What a people? Their values appeared to be inside out. Back home, people placed so much value on human warmth in spite of their extremely warm climate but these people with their harsh cold climate did not seem to care about the warmth from other human beings. No wonder some of them would prefer to make cats and dogs the beneficiaries of their property whereas there were human beings around them that lived like the birds of the air, that brave very cold winters in fragile nests or like foxes that live in holes. Those who bother to have children hasten to send them away as soon they approached adulthood. Dion wondered as he wandered towards his flat. When he put the key of his door lock into its hole, he thought aloud, *different places, different climates.*

Chapter Eight

*I*t was a pretty long time that Dion had not gone to 48, Chancellor street, Cannon Park. He thought that another visit there would be refreshing. It would be fun to meet someone like Tom Jones, occasionally, in order to hear him talk about good old Cameroon. A country that he had crossed many rivers and seas to go to and defend, on behalf of Her Majesty the Queen. But because the young shall grow, that country has evolved and kept aside the *Union Jack* and stopped singing *God Save the Queen*, in order to take its destiny into its own hands. And indeed it has, as it has consistently grappled with the things it takes for a nation to enjoy its sovereignty. Dion called him and took an appointment to visit him. He had since learnt that different places had their different climates. Back home it was quite normal to visit anyone, especially the elderly, without a prior warning.

While walking gently towards Cannon Park, he got very excited about meeting his host. Ever since he got to England, he had not read a single leaflet on the acquired immune deficiency syndrome (AIDS), yet in his country it was such a scare, nobody with a concerned mind could have quiet sleep at night. Every little community had its HIV/AIDS vigilante group. He had observed that the concept did not seem to be a bother to his host country and he thought he should talk about it to Tom Jones, hoping that he was likely to know something about it. Shortly before he left his country, the question of AIDS was a big, big bang.

People were so excited about it that mother earth seemed to have stood still for a moment and then started revolving around it. It was like a bolt from the blue, that had taken people unawares and they were dying in their thousands. It was stunningly scary, as each one only counted their days. Young girls Dion had grown up with were caught up one by one by the deadly disease and in a space of three years all the village beauties were gone. People were so scared they could not call it by its name and so they started calling it six plus two or five plus three. As soon as anyone started losing weight, the public verdict was they had contracted six plus two. The general assumption was that God had become impatient with the wrongs of humanity and had sent down this illness in his anger to humiliate and wipe out the human race. Other people speculated that it had nothing to do with God. It had originated from black Africans, who had occult dealings with monkeys and chimpanzees. And yet others said it had nothing to do with Africans, it had resulted from a deviant practice called homosexuality. Still, there were some people who speculated that it was a creation of some evil scientists whose tendency for self destruction did not end with themselves but had to extend to the whole human race. They were said to have created the Human Immune Virus to be injected into every human being through the most reliable source – sex. Amid all this confusion, some people thought that several plagues had come and gone. This could just be one of them, so instead of wild speculations, humans should rather put their heads together and seek a solution.

Before Dion came to England a way had been found on how to identify who had been infected and who had not. People had started being tested for HIV infection, although some of the persons found to be positive had been treated like lepers. Because of this many of them had committed suicide or precipitated their deaths by severing their links with the will to live. It was a very serious matter back home and yet he had observed that it was handled with so much equanimity there in the U.K. As a matter of fact, he expected to have been tested for the infection before he entered their country but this was not done. He was going to find out from Tom Jones the reason for such level-headedness towards the pandemic.

When he got to Tom's home he was very busy with Lisa.

"How's Lisa doing Tom?" Dion asked.

"Wonderful! She's a wonderful machine."

"You mean wife."

"Ah yes, she's a wonderful wife. Very serviceable." Said Tom.

"Glad to hear that." Dion said, with a feeling of assurance.

"Now, what do I offer you? Tea or coffee."

"Tea please."

"Good. And tell you what? I've got some tea from your country."

"Tea from my country? What's that?"

"Have a look!"

Dion threw his eyes on the packet and the label read *Tole Tea*.

"Tole Tea! Where did you get it from?"

"Holland Park in London."

"Holland Park, Holland Park," Dion tried to remember.

"That's where your country's eh –m High Commission is."

"I see. Was the tea being sold there?"

"No, I found myself at Holland Park and then I saw a flag with colours: green, red and then yellow, fluttering against a building. When I looked closely I found out it was the High Commission of your country. Out of curiosity I walked in there and introduced myself. One of the officials was very welcoming. He took me round and we had a friendly chat, at the end of which he offered me the tea. I was very pleased with the present and I had kept some for you, in case you visit. And here you are enjoying the flavour of home grown tea in a strange land."

"Thanks for the concern Tom. I'm really very delighted to drink tea from my home. You cannot imagine how I feel right now. It's like I'm right there in Buea on a foggy day, driving downhill to the enigmatic village of Sasse going through the tea fields as men and women in rather ragged clothing are harvesting the tender leaves and piling them in the large baskets mounted on their bent backs. I'm so glad to know that what we produce in my country can be appreciated here. Tom, I'm so, so happy."

"I can understand your feelings boy. What surprises me is that you can't find the tea in any of our shops, here."

"It's such a wonder for me too, Tom. I go to Tesco for fresh food and I find bananas from the Bahamas, or plantains from Trinidad and none of such products from my country. And they are back there at home rotting in the wilds."

"Never mind boy, things will change."

"I hope they do," Tom said doubtfully.

Dion took his tea silently as Tom finished up the work he was doing on the computer. By the time Tom crossed over to grab a cup himself he had already gulped down four. When he noticed that Tom was looking at him with questioning eyes, he addressed him:

"Why's your country so silent about this thing they call AIDS."

"Aid! You mean aid to developing countries, like yours?"

No, that's not what I mean. I'm talking about AIDs – Acquired Immune Deficiency Syndrome."

"I understand. But what do you mean silent?"

"Nobody seems to talk about it, nor even worry about it. For example, ever since I got here I've not received any leaflet educating me about it. Whereas back home, the song: CFA is common currency."

"What's CFA?"

"C - for condom
 F - for fidelity

A - for abstinence. That's the hit song back home. Condoms that used to be a very private commodity are now sold everywhere and even distributed free of charge. Parents are forever answering questions from their children about them."

"Well Dion, talking about silence on AIDS, I don't think we are. I guess you haven't been to hospital ever since you came here."

"Of course I have. When I went there to look for you."

"Oh, when you came to look for me, a patient. In that case you had been to the hospital, not been to hospital."

"What difference does it make?"

"The difference, my boy is that when you go to hospital, you're a patient. But when you go to the hospital, you're not there for the service of the institution. You're a passerby or you're visiting. So I had guessed rightly that you hadn't been to hospital ever since you got here. If you had, you would probably have been given information about AIDS. The population here is so educated, there isn't much need for sustained campaigns on such issues, like AIDS and besides, the idea has been with us for quite a long time. That explains the reason why you believe that the society is silent on the AIDS issue."

"Tom, I'm saying so because the situation is really alarming in my country. Three quarters of the NGOs back there are involved in AIDS - centred activities. Besides, the concept of AIDS has only recently been uncovered and very few people have come to terms with it."

"In that case, vigorous campaigns against the disease are absolutely justified and given the level of education of your people, the campaigns should go on for a long time." Said Tom Jones with much conviction.

"You're right Tom. Many people refuse to accept the reality of AIDS. Come to think of it, there was this young medical student, called Ndutu. He was in the third year and he watched his health deteriorating gradually. He had constant headaches and fever, which had hardly been the case with him. He usually treated them himself and moved on with life. Shortly after, he started losing weight. When his friends complained he said he had been watching his weight recently. By the time he went to the fourth year, things were getting worse for him. Instead of going in for medical laboratory tests to help diagnose his health problem he preferred to go to a traditional healer. In order to carry out a diagnosis, the healer did his tests in his temple. Here, the patient sat on a stool and a basin of water is put in front of him. He requested Ndutu to dip in a five hundred francs coin. Having done this, he recited so many incantations behold the head of an old woman appeared in the basin of water. It looked very frightful but Ndutu held his grounds. The head looked at him straight in the eyes and he too looked at it steadily. Shortly a voice was heard:

"My son, what do you want here?"

"Your ladyship, I want information about my health."

"Good. You're at the right place. How long have you been ill?"

"Your ladyship, I thought you should know that already."

"Yes, I should but I want confirmation from you. And please, have it in your head that I know why I ask certain questions and say certain things. So tell me how long you've been ill."

"For about thirteen months."

"Young man, you're very lucky to have come here now. You happen to be the first person in your family and in fact the entire village to become a student in a medical school. You have only a few years to become a medical doctor and the people don't like it. They don't think that of all families in your village, yours should be the one to produce a medical doctor. So they are determined to do away with you. That's the only way to suppress their jealousy, wiping you out of existence. So you have been bewitched by them and you are dying slowly." The voice said and faded out. The head too disappeared suddenly from the basin of water.

Ndutu was stunned by the spectacle and especially the words: *you are dying slowly*. He thought about these people who had taken him for their celebrity. They hailed him as their doctor to be and everywhere he went he was welcomed with open hands and highly appreciated. He wondered how the same people would want him dead. If he died the hope of having a single doctor who comes from that village would be shattered. And how would they feel? Ndutu pondered over so many questions that could not be answered. He turned to the traditional healer and asked:

"What next?"

"The treatment," he replied.

"What does it take?"

"First you'd have to commune with your ancestors. They must know what's going on. You'd provide a white goat and a big bunch of plantains. Two cobs of maize, and half a litre of palm oil. Then you will arrange for my transport to the village, where the traditional rites of giving food to the ancestors will be performed. After that we shall start the second phase of the treatment."

Chapter Nine

*N*dutu provided the requirements and he and the traditional healer went to their village. He called his immediate family and explained to them what he had diagnosed and the treatment he had planned for their son. They all agreed that the village people were very jealous and they were capable of such evil. Such jealousy was the cause of the backwardness experienced there. They arranged that the rites would be performed the following day at the first cockcrow.

The family went to bed keen on getting up as soon as they heard the first crows of the cocks. Ndutu himself was very tired and he was not sure that the cock's crows would get him up and indeed they could not. When the time came, it was one of his cousins who stood over him and shook him vigorously to get up. He got up very reluctantly and staggered his way to the water pot. He took out a cup full of water, went outside and washed his face to drive away sleep. He then went and joined the rest of the family that was already sitting in a semi-circle under the plum tree in the middle of the yard. He was given a seat in front of every body. The healer, Akwanka was his name, then walked up to him and poured some black palm kernel oil on his head, which had earlier been laid bare of its hair. He rubbed it vigorously while reciting incantations, moving down to his face and then his chest. After the exercise he said he had cleansed Ndutu of all evil. He requested each member of the family to place their two palms on his head in turns, and pronounce the words *barem ambaka ne woh, banki roh booh mek bananga ne woh*. These words translated the gods be with you, they shouldn't let earth's children destroy you. After each of them had taken their turn, Akwanka led the group in a prayer that lasted thirty minutes. After the prayer, the white goat was slaughtered and some of the fresh blood that spurted out of the slashed neck was collected in a bowl. Akwanka drank from the bowl and passed it over to Ndutu. He entreated him to drink and he drank all of it. The goat was butchered and given out to be prepared along with the bunch of plantains. Before the day broke completely, the maize was grilled in grains and some of the sauce from the pot of goat meat, palm oil, some of the boiled plantains and the grains of maize were all mixed and taken to the family shrine at the foot of a mighty cotton tree. The food was left there for the ancestors and the living sat back under the plum tree and each had their own share of the food. They ate, drank palm wine and dispersed before the sun rose.

This was the first part of Ndutu's treatment. The healer was to go back to town with him and carry out the second phase, which had to do with different roots including fresh ginseng roots steeped in *afofo*, a locally brewed gin.

Somehow Ndutu was getting better and stronger. As he kept improving, so did Akwanka's idea that some of the jealous people in his village were after his life. He made up his mind to steer clear of them, even though it meant losing his roots. After four months, Ndutu was able to go back to school and write the exams which qualified him for the fifth year. He was very grateful to Akwanka, who had convinced him that traditional medicine was complementary to medical science. However, six months after he thought he had been treated, he started feeling bad again. His headaches returned, persistent coughs and fever had returned fully. He went back to Akwanka, who did all he could to help him. He even kept him in his healing home and month after month, his condition was deteriorating. Finally, Ndutu realized that he was going no where as far as his health was concerned. He realized that it was ridiculous for him to be training as a medical doctor and dying from a medical problem. If Akwanka could treat headaches, fevers and coughs mysteriously put in him by jealous people, why should medical science not do the same. He wondered why in the first place, he got hooked up to Akwanka. As things got worse, he decided to do what he dreaded – consult a medical doctor. He, Ndutu, a doctor to be, to display himself in public as a patient was unthinkable. This explained why he got hooked to Akwanka.

"Why did I get so hooked to that man?" he thought. After reflecting over the matter, he said to himself:

I do realize my problem is a great lack of humility and yet the bible says in the gospel of Saint Matthew, *Blessed are the meek: for they shall inherit the earth.* Inheriting the earth is surely living longer on it. So we should be humble, in order to hang around for quite a while. Tomorrow, I'll throw pride and arrogance overboard and go to consult a medical doctor."

The following day, Ndutu kept his promise, he went to consult a doctor. After careful examination the doctor asked him to go and do a number of tests, one of which included an HIV test.

"Why an HIV test doctor?" He inquired.

"To know your status and treat you accordingly. The test may not be necessary if you provide evidence of your status."

"I have no evidence, but I should voluntarily request to do it. You can't impose it on me, can you?"

"I can't but now you're my patient and I have to find out what's wrong with you. In this case by all means, including your HIV status."

"You win doctor. Humility brought me to this and so will it take me to the end." Ndutu said regretfully.

Ndutu went to a well-known medical laboratory- *Laboratoire de Biyem-assi* located in the neighbourhood of Biyem-assi in Yaounde. He submitted the doctor's request for tests. After a few minutes, he was ushered into a cubicle where his blood sample was taken. He was requested to return in two hours. As he stepped out of the premises of the laboratory he thought aloud:

"One thing I don't like about tests is that most of the time, the test results are said to be negative, therefore the expenditure on them is a waste of resources".

When he returned for the results, three of them were ready and this time all of them were positive. That of HIV was not ready and he was asked to come the following day. He went away very disappointed. He had become anxious about his status and he thought all was going to be settled that hour. Unfortunately, that wasn't the case. He still had at least twenty-four hours to wait. As for the other results, for the first time he had not wasted his money, they were all positive; which meant, they found what they were looking for. He wondered whether to hope that the result he was still expecting should be negative or positive. If it indicated negative then the doctor would not have found what he was looking for - the human immune-deficiency virus, and his life would go on as usual. But if it indicated positive, then the root cause of all his ailments would have been found and the doctors would take the necessary measures to deal with the situation. But how effective would their measures be? That's the question. Yes it was the question that Ndutu pondered over:

"AIDS, the offshoot of HIV," he thought, "is known to be a devastating disease because it almost always ends in death. It had not been around much but millions of people had taken their leave off the stage because of it. Many are those who had collapsed and died simply by spelling out the word positive in their test result notification. Others had simply given up the will to live. Some had fought bravely

66

with the devastating effects but had run short of the means and died. What will my case be when *positive* appears on the notification? I know *negative* will be good but things will still be unclear as I will still be ill, very ill. I decided, I will wait and see."

he following day, Ndutu was at the doorsteps of *Laboratoire de Biyem-assi* at 2.00 p.m. He walked straight to the cubicle in which his blood sample had been taken. He found the attendant who had attended to him the previous day. She sent him to the psychologist. As he got in there he understood everything. He needed to be counseled. He told the psychologist that he did not need any counseling. He was a medical student himself and he had prepared himself psychologically for the result. In that case, the white envelope was handed to him. He folded it and put it in his breast pocket. He thanked the psychologist and walked out. He opened the envelope only after he had got home. It confirmed his expectations and he had to reflect on the next plan of action.

He saw his present slip beneath his feet and his future crumble like a rotten pumpkin beneath a frustrated foot. When he entered the medical school four years ago, it was clear to him that he had arrived. Getting into a medical school was very competitive. The competition was a triangular combination of brain, luck and cash. The dire lack of cash was a great handicap for him but he went into the competition relying on brain and luck. The two were quite dependable as he got a place in the medical school. Since the day he entered the school, his shoulders went up, high. The future had opened up like a dual carriageway with each way having triple lanes. He could not envisage any obstacle. He trusted himself, as far

68

as brainwork was concerned and he knew there would be no doubt he too would be called Doctor Ndutu – a holder of a key that opens all doors and why not all hearts. He looked at his test results once again and shrugged his shoulders. He had been moving about keeping them high, henceforth he would move about keeping them low. Quite understandable because his life was over, and invariably his dreams. He had become very susceptible to death and he could say his adieux anytime. He decided he would take the result to the doctor the following day. When he went to bed, he surprisingly fell asleep. In his sleep he dreamt that he had a confrontation with an eagle. It was big and strong. He fought courageously with it but it beat him in the fight. When he was on the brink of raising his arms in surrender, the eagle grabbed them and flew off. In the twinkle of an eye they were far up in the sky. When he managed to look downward he realised that he would be pieces of meat for any passing carnivore in case the eagle let go its grip. It kept going up, up and up until it got to a spot with bright lights. He started circling and circling and suddenly it loosened its grip on Ndutu. He thought his end had come but he instead landed on soft cushions. When he looked around him he saw a beautifully furnished living room.

"This must be heaven," he murmured.

"Yes you're in heaven." a sweet voice intoned.

"Me, in heaven. How can that be?"

"Yes, it is. The eagle has brought you to heaven. Lucky you. And very soon you'd be flanked by seven virgins. Beautiful virgins. Three on your right side, and three others on your left. One will be standing directly behind you, massaging your back, shoulders and neck, using her delicate fingers"

"And what will I do with them?"

"Marry them of course. Virgins are supposed to be married by any marriageable man or are you not a man?"

"Of course I am. Only …"

"Only what?"

"Only I've just been tested HIV positive."

"What's that supposed to mean?"

"It means, it means that I have human immune-deficiency virus, which eats up my blood cells and weakens my immune system, subjecting me to a syndrome called AIDS. If I marry these virgins I shall infect them all and one by one, they will die along with me."

"Did I hear you say die?"

"Yes, I said die."

"Shut up! There's no such word here. You are on very holy ground – Heaven. You have been infected by HIV."

"But that's what I've just told you."

"Quiet! The HIV here is different from the trash you said you got from down there. Up here you've been infected by Heaven Immune Virus. Which gives you immunity to everything including death. That's why I said the word die doesn't exist here. Do you understand me now?"

"Yes I do. So you mean, I've got no problem and I can go ahead and marry these seven very beautiful virgins. How wonderful, oh how wonderful is it to find yourself in heaven." He shouted with much delight, which made him open his eyes.

Ndutu rubbed his eyes and looked around him. He realized that he had been dreaming. He looked at his watch and noticed that it was quarter to five in the morning. He thought about the dream and then about the long day in front of him. The rest of the day came on gradually and he went to keep his appointment with the doctor.

"Yes Ndutu, let's have a go at your test result," the doctor said cheerfully.

Ndutu handed him the envelope, not feeling amused.

"Considering that it's not sealed I guess your result is already known to you."

"Yes doctor."

"So, you don't need any counseling, do you?"

"No."

The doctor spread the paper out and read the result silently, nodding his head as if to confirm his fears. He took up his head, looked at Ndutu and said:

"Right. You'd go for more tests. We shall like to find out your CD4 count to enable us know how badly you've been infected."

"At your disposal doctor. A ripe banana can't be afraid of getting rotten."

"That's being pessimistic, Ndutu. There're people living with AIDS and they don't consider themselves as bananas that will soon get rotten."

"You're right doctor. It depends on the person. I cannot pretend to be up when I know I'm down."

"All right, all right. You're entitled to your beliefs, but try not to give up foolishly."

Ndutu went and did his CD4 count and the doctor placed him on the famous tri-therapy after educating him on how to live with AIDS. After three months on the treatment, Ndutu started regaining his strength and carried out his work in the medical school effectively. He easily got back to life and started questioning the truth about the idea that his health problems had been caused by his own people in the village. He thought that Akwanka's diagnoses had been plausible but his treatment had cast doubts on them. Good diagnosis should be a harbinger of good treatment. Since the treatment had been ineffective the diagnoses too must be defective. He tried to re-examine the rationale in eliminating the only doctor an entire community was going to have. He concluded that the people could be jealous but their jealousy would not go to the extent of spilling blood.

So he considered that he had gone blind of reason in the face of his problems. And in his present circumstances, he was somehow feeling fine but at the expense of so much money. He had been on a scholarship allowance ever since he entered the medical school and he had been saving half of it to give himself financial security as he proceeded with his education. His tri-therapy had depleted a lot of the savings. So he was wondering what would happen by the time the last franc might have been spent. He still had two years to complete his medical studies and his allowance was only good enough to sustain a healthy student. He had accepted his fate but his problem was the wherewithal to stay alive. He had known people who had been financially ruined because of the high cost of servicing their AIDS condition and because of this they ended up dying. He wondered if he too would die by the time he wouldn't have money to buy the tri-therapy. It was at this point that he thought of Josephine alias Jojo, a girl whose dream had been to marry a medical doctor and ever since he became a medical student, this girl had targeted him for friendship. He had been very elusive because he did not have any feeling, sentimental feeling for her. They had however, continued to be acquaintances. After Jojo's first degree which was in Accountancy, she easily found a job with a multinational company. She was handsomely remunerated and she was living well. Ndutu felt that the only opportunity left for him to sustain his life was to get Jojo to marry him. He revisited her in his mind's eye and saw in her an exceedingly beautiful woman, almost one metre seventy-five centimeters tall, holding herself gracefully with a permanent smile that drew attention to her medium-sized lips that were a great attraction for spontaneous kisses. She spoke softly and sweetly to anyone who cared to listen. Ndutu wondered why he had been so passive towards her. He thought whether it was because she had so openly shown that she had got the hot pants for him that put him off. It was time to give her some attention. So he deliberately got himself in her way and she thought she was the luckiest girl on the planet to have found Ndutu in her snare, at last. It did not take both of them long to go steady. Six months later Jojo was pregnant and her happiness was in more than superlative terms. Ndutu on the other hand knew that there would be problems very soon. All along he had been taking his drugs discreetly and Josephine hadn't the faintest idea that he was HIV positive. So when she started her pre-natal consultations, one of the tests the gynaecologist had requested her to do was the HIV. When she returned home she was very worried. She wondered about the result and how first, she would take it and then Ndutu if it happened to be positive. Then Ndutu walked in. As soon as they finished having lunch, Josephine called Ndutu's attention with a slight cough and then said, "honey, I've begun the pre-natal consultations today you know?"

"So, you have!" Ndutu exclaimed.

"Yes, indeed."

"And what's up?"

"Among the tests that I"ve been asked to do, one is the HIV test and I'm scared stiff. This HIV of a thing has come to send everyone into a mini hell before the real hell. Just before I had completely savoured the pleasure of getting pregnant by the man I want, along comes the threat of HIV. Well, Ndutu we have no choice but to face it. The doctor says it's for the good of the unborn baby. It's good for it to know its status before it's born. So, shall we go for the test both of us?"

"There'd be no need. You go and do it, as requested by the doctor. When you get the result we shall get to manage it together."

Ndutu already knew the outcome of the results. He wondered how Jojo would take it. She had been very understanding and kind to him as a girlfriend. He on the other hand, had been caring although he had not had the courage to discuss his status with her. And then a pregnancy had resulted and the foetus was about six weeks old. It was crucial to know how Jojo would react to the result but there was nothing he could do about it.

Jojo went for her test three days later and got the results four days after. It was a stunning revelation and she was at a loss on what to do next. She went down memory lane, trying to work out who among the men she had slept with before meeting Ndutu might have caused the damage. Having struggled in vain to hook up Ndutu, in order to fulfill her pet dream of having a doctor husband, she had given up in order to try her luck anywhere, especially because time was running out. And given the lucrative job that she had, the men had been tumbling over one another to get at her. Unfortunately, none of them was a medical doctor, which made her go into several trial periods. After a good number of such periods, she was about to make up her mind about one of them, when along came Ndutu. She did not even have the time to ask herself why the dramatic volte-face on his part. She simply fell headlong for him and then the pregnancy. They had not even found time to discuss marriage. She had not taken the matter seriously because she felt that with a baby between them marriage was assured. And then, there's the stigma, the HIV stigma. Who might have done this to her? She had even lost count of the number of men she had slept with and so it was difficult to say who was who. Her mind could hardly go to her darling doctor man. It couldn't be him - a man in the medical profession. They who are in the central committee of the medical profession would not get into the mistake of being infected by HIV. She wondered how she was going to face him. And the little boy or girl in her womb, was going to be born with an infection that they knew nothing of. Poor child, he or she would start living with AIDS from birth. She kept wondering about who might have done this to her and then her mind went to one of the few married men that she had fallen victim to. She knew she did not have any future with men who already had their dear wives but somehow, being vulnerable some of such men ran into her and had their go. One of them was this flamboyant high ranking police officer who didn't think any single person in skirt wasn't meant for his consumption. She had always been one of the proud girls who went about with her head high and peacocks like the flamboyant police officer would easily put her off, but some how he didn't and she succumbed. And one by one the girls who had been his victims had died and two years after he himself died. Since then she had been so scared to do the test, in case she was tested positive. She preferred to live in ignorance, rather then get the sentence. Occasionally, she was consoled by the fact that the police officer's wife was still alive and strong. It was a wonder that her husband had imposed the death sentence on many a woman and she was still hale and hearty. So, she too might be save and she had lived with this idea all along, until the pregnancy, Ndutu's baby. All her dreams, her sweet dreams had been shattered by a single word: *positive*.

hen Jojo got home that day, she did everything to look happy. But forced happiness like everything thing that is done forcefully is difficult to hide from a discerning eye. Ndutu noticed that she was not her usual self when she walked in. He had been home and he had for once got the lunch ready. He set the table and they sat to eat.

"So you can be such a good cook Ndutu," Jojo said passively.

"Of course yes. Having been single all my life, I had no option but learn how to cook. You had never given me a chance to cook for you that's why you're only realizing it now."

"Now that I know, I wish I could give you a lot more chances to cook," she said softly.

"I'm at your disposal anytime my work doesn't tie me down. And the baby, how is it kicking?"

"It's such a lazy baby, it doesn't do any kicking."

"That's like the father. No stress."

"I hope it is alive anyway."

"Why not? Why am I training to be a doctor if my own baby can't stay alive? Come over here, let me examine you."

At this point, Jojo became very emotional and she could not hold her tears. When Ndutu noticed them, he knew the bitter truth had been told her.

"Come on Jojo, is it the result?" he whispered.

"No, the result isn't ready yet. I've been asked to come by in two days."

"So, what's making you moody?"

"The fact that our baby will be born out of wedlock."

"Do you take that for a problem? If you do, then *ashia*. My baby is my baby whether it is born in or out of wedlock. We can't get into the hurdle of a wedding simply because we're expecting a baby. As far as I'm concerned, you're going to be my wife, whether it takes the next decade or two, I have no problem. I'm already carrying out my functions, aren't I?"

"Yes, you are. I can see that but I need to be called Mrs. Josephine Ndutu before anything happens to me."

"Are you expecting anything to happen to you?"

"I'm not, but one never knows."

"I hate to live in doubts. I would like to believe in myself and trust that the one who caused me to be on this earth has his reason for doing so. Can you turn around so I can find out how the baby's doing?"

Jojo turned around and with his stethoscope, Ndutu examined her and assured her that her baby was doing fine. Later she cleared the table and had the dishes washed and dried. He left for his own home after they had watched a couple of films on TV together. At nine p.m. Jojo went to bed. She had lied to Ndutu about the result of the test. She did not have the courage to tell him. She was very convinced that she had been infected by the reckless police officer and the consequence was a shattered life for her. She knew of the tri-therapy and with it she could still carry on with her life for a pretty long time and above all she could support the cost. But her problem was Ndutu. She had infected him and the baby. She wondered how she was going to live with such guilt, even if Ndutu forgave her. Jojo rolled from one side of her bed to the other until the small hours of the morning. When she closed her eyes, she heard wedding bells, ushering her to the grand cathedral of the city. Ndutu had graduated and was a very prominent doctor. A cardiologist of international reputation. He had had a number of successes including the transplanting of the hearts of two presidents whose hearts had been exhausted by three decades of service to their people. He had got the highest honours from these statesmen as they continued to rule their respective nations. This wedding was attended by them and other dignitaries from around the world. She was at her best and she thanked God who had given her the wisdom to make the right choice. Her parents who had blamed her for running behind a mere student, who had nothing to offer, were full of joy. One of the flower girls was their own daughter. The most beautiful girl she had ever set her eyes on.

When she got to the entrance of the cathedral, she heard a solemn song of Hendel's gently spilling out of the loud speakers. As she stepped in, everybody present including the Heads of Government were on their feet. She was walking up to the altar at a gentle pace to take the hand of her Ndutu. "Oh what other heaven did one expect!" she exclaimed and got up. She realised she was dreaming.

"O what a dream," she murmured. "Can this come to pass?"

"So, my baby was going to be a girl. The most beautiful girl that existence had ever known. Will she come to pass? No way. HIV has done its worse." She concluded and got up from bed.

On his part, Ndutu had returned to his home wondering whether he had done the right thing to have left Jojo by herself. Even though she had not yet received the result of the test, she seemed to be worried about the outcome. It was stupid of him not to stay and console her. But at the same time, he would have implicated himself and where was that going to lead him to, he wondered. Two more days for her to receive the bombshell and this meant two more days for him to receive her reaction. He wondered whether she was going to explode like a bomb and cause a crater lake in his heart. He hoped that it would not get to that extent. He would like to see his baby, safely born and he would like to see it live like other children, HIV or no HIV. He was already living with it and by God's grace, he would fulfill his ambition – that of becoming a medical doctor. He decided he would size up Jojo's reaction and then come up with a solution.

In the morning, she rushed there and prepared the breakfast before going to school. She ate her breakfast and left for work. She worked very hard that day, ridding her table of all the files that were pending. Ndutu was surprised that she had worked that late. She came back very exhausted and was pleased to find that Ndutu had prepared the dinner. They ate in silence and when they had finished, she opted to clear the table and do the dishes. When he protested, asking her to go and rest, she said she wanted to perform her last duties of a housewife.

"What do you mean, last duties?" Ndutu asked.

"I mean my last duties as your wife."

"Do you mean I'll dump you if the result is sero-positive?"

"One never knows. The world in its very nature turns round and round."

"I see. So, you don't trust me?"

"If I didn't, I woudn't be hoping you'd marry me."

"Rest assured, Jojo, whatever might be the outcome of the result I'd not let you down."

"Good to hear that baby as it reminds me of the Beatles' hit song *Don't Let Me Down*."

"Sure baby I won't let you down and to prove that I'm going to spend the night here with my baby. All the assignments will have to wait."

"Dear, if you've got assignments you'd better go and do them. I'll take care of myself. Remember it's tomorrow that I'll go for the test result. I'll need you more after I'd have had the result. So be a good boy and go and do your assignments. Try not to have any assignments tomorrow, for you'd have no excuse for sleeping away from my bed."

"Ok! I've heard you. Take care and have a lovely night. I'll be around to get your breakfast ready," Ndutu said and kissed her goodnight.

When he left, she securely locked the main door and took out the key. Then she taught of the last supper. It was true she had just had supper prepared by Ndutu but she had forgotten to tell him it was her last supper. So she was going to have her last supper all by herself. She felt very sorry for Ndutu. She lured him into falling in love with her. It was true that he had been the one who had run after her in the last moment but she had initiated and encouraged him all along and finally, injected the deadly virus in him and his baby.

"What a shame!" she wept. "Only a shameless person would stand such a shameful situation."

She wept, and wept for over an hour. Then she decided to take a pen and a piece of paper to leave a note for Ndutu.

> Ndutu is the love I've known ever since I was born
> But he didn't give me a chance, even
> To express it. My desperate attempts to catch his eye
> Fell on ice, and when the ice melted, it took away
> My endeavours and my yearning, for decent love.
> I ran riot into riotous love, like a dove
> Whose way missed, got into a cage.
> And see what I've got to- a deadly stage.
> A sting that's stung my love and all I have.
> Too late you came Ndutu –See what I've got.
> A deadly sting that's stung you and all I've got.

When she had finished writing, she placed it on the table in her living room and put the key of her main door on it to prevent the paper from flying off in case there was the slightest breeze. She then went to the kitchen and got some garri into a small bowl and had it soaked in cold water. She put some sugar in the bowl to sweeten the stuff. Then she picked up her red handbag and took out a small plastic pack. It was half full of rat poison locally called *arata die*. She emptied the pack in the bowl, stirred it gently and then sat down to have her last supper. The effect was devastating. It wasn't quite ten minutes when life, the sweet life she had looked forward to, slipped out of her, and her alluring lips were clipped for good. The bowl still had much of the deadly stuff.

The morning was peaceful. No rain, no winds, no fog. Ndutu had decided to walk to Jojo's flat. It took him only fifteen minutes to get there. He knocked, in the hope that there would be a response within but there was none. He felt that it was understandable. Jojo had worked so hard the previous day, so she ought to be very tired and had the right to get up late. He tried again but still no response. He dipped his hands into his pockets to see if he had brought the spare key that he kept and there was none. He knocked again and again but again and again there was no reply. He decided to go for the spare key, so it was thirty minutes later that the truth poured down on him like holy ghost fire. She lay back up, in the lone sofa in the living room. He wondered if the baby in her, had caused it. No, it couldn't be. Innocent little thing. It could not kick hard, in the hope not to hurt. How then could it cause a thing as cruel as death.

"Oh Ndutu," he exclaimed, "when shall my troubles end?"

His eyes fell on the key and then the paper that it protected. He quickly picked it up and his eyes consumed the content.

"So, I did it! I caused this disaster!" he cried. "And this angel lying here thought it was her sting that had caused it. How I wish I could catch up with her and tell her the sting is me, this worthless me. She told me everything but I refused to understand. She told me to go and do my homework and I foolishly left. I must rush after her, my angel."

When he uttered the word angel, his dream of seven angels came back to him. Could it not be possible that it was time his dream came true. Only the Angels offered him in heaven were all white. He did not see any black one but he could possibly make a special request for a black one. They might not refuse him that singular request and he was sure Jojo would be that one. His eyes turned to the stuff in the bowl on the table. He immediately knew what it was made of. He decided to act fast, before he was invaded by second thoughts. He picked up the spoon that Jojo had used, filled it and then got his mouth full. He swallowed and got another spoonful. His mind quickly went back to his dream but before he could remember how it all began, everything went blank.

"So, Tom, you see what HIV/AIDS has done and is doing to my country. There are thousands of Ndutus and Jojos back home. As a matter of fact an entire nation has been caught pants down," Dion said desperately.

"It's a pity Dion. However, it is widely believed that experience is the best teacher. I do hope that the experience that your country is going through will be good lessons to be learnt, even if they are at the cost of human lives. Humanity has learned huge lessons from the hugest human disasters – the world wars. It is my hope that the lessons your people are learning from the present experiences will make them better managers of crises. One thing people should learn to accept is to live with perpetual danger. It was a French man called Corneille who said that *we triumph without glory when we conquer without danger*. It is true that values are different from place to place. But there should be universal values as there are universal problems. I'll tell you how here in England a couple accepted each other and lived their lives amidst the danger of dying of AIDS."

"Are they still alive?" asked Dion.

"Yes, they are."

"How far are they from here."

"Not quite far. At Kenilworth. One of the towns that you feared would be destroyed by your amulet transformed into a bomb."

"Well Tom, let's forget about my amulet. For now it's a bygone. Besides, it became impotent because it was raped by your dog."

"My poor dog. It can't defend itself. So it takes the blame."

"Anyway, what are the names of this couple."

"Steve and Annie Bottomless."

"Bottomless. A very unusual surname."

"Sounds unusual because you haven't heard it before. But there are as many Bottomlesses as there are Bushes and Bullocks around here."

Chapter Twelve

"Annie Parker, so she was called before she married Steve Bottomless, used to be the girl every young man wanted to associate with" Tom said, looking excited. "She was down-to-earth, intelligent, resourceful and inspiring. Above these pleasant qualities, she was a piece of elegance. Her oval face that carried all the other parts, proportionately put in place, seemed to sit gracefully on an exquisite neck above her shoulders. The hair that capped her was gold. She was a metre sixty tall and she walked with such grace, one would think she was a descendant of Elizabeth II. At nineteen she had admission to read Law in Warwick University, your university. A year before graduation, a friend invited her to go for shopping at one of the malls in Birmingham. On their way back, her friend who was behind the steering wheel, suddenly lost concentration and the car skidded off the road and hit an embankment. Her friend died on the spot and Annie barely survived. She had multiple fractures and deep wounds on her face and other parts of her body. By the time she was in hospital, she had lost consciousness from profuse bleeding. Lucky girl, she got out of hospital after six months but she was an antithesis of the Annie everyone around her had known. She had a scar on her forehead and a twist on her nose. She, however, had to go on with her life. She returned to the university to end her course and start a career in banking. She had a job in the local branch of

Barclays in Kenilworth. She was gradually picking up the pieces of her shattered life. She had not only been scared physically but also morally. Several months after leaving the hospital, she did a routine HIV test and she was found to be sero-positive. She found this very embarrassing as she had been a very careful person as far as sex habits were concerned. A second test confirmed this status and it was quite devastating, especially because she could hardly conjecture how the virus got at her. However, she concluded that having been an accident patient needing blood transfusion and so much surgery, anything might have happened. She simply swallowed the pill and told herself that life had to continue.

Annie usually spent her weekends receiving her well-wishers, who did not cease to visit her and encourage her to push on. Many of whom had been her friends at the university and family relatives. One weekend, in a cold winter Saturday evening, a tall dark gentleman in his thirties rang Annie's doorbell. When she opened, it wasn't one of the usual faces that stood facing her. It was a complete stranger but he looked genuinely friendly and also very attractive. She was embarrassed and so stood still for a few seconds. Then she thought she should ask him in.

"Come in."

"Thank you," he said as he walked in.

"Can I take your coat?"

"Of course," he answered as he handed the coat to her.

"Have a seat."

"Thank you. It's pleasantly warm here. You've got quite a cozy place."

"Thank you."

"You're Parker. Annie Parker, aren't you?"

"Yes, I am."

"I'm Steve. Steve Bottomless."

"Hello Steve. It's a pleasure for you to visit me like this."

"The pleasure's all mine. I'm sorry I just ran into you like that. I live only a couple of blocks from you, so out of curiosity, I decided to walk here and visit."

"That's all right. You want some coffee or tea?"

"Coffee, please."

Annie turned her back and walked to the kitchen. As she did she felt the bright eyes of Steve watching her every step. Instinctively, she turned her head and shot a glance at him over her left shoulder. She caught his eye. He was actually following her every step. She wondered whether the wretched soul that she had become could have a place in the heart of such a handsome man. She took his gestures for mere curiosity. Five minutes later, she returned with two hot coffees and extended her right hand to him.

"Here you are, Steve"

"Thanks a lot"

At first they sipped their coffee in silence but a few minutes later, Annie broke the silence.

"Where do you work, Steve?"

"I'm a broker. An insurance broker."

"Oh that's interesting. I got used to the insurance business after my accident."

"Yeah. I can see the effects of the accident. The breaking down of much of the beauty."

"Oh Steve. Let's not talk about that. It brings back horrible memories, especially the death of Diana, my friend who was driving. I'm lucky. All I've lost is beauty."

"Never, mind love. The beauty is still there. In my mind's eye."

"You crazy?"

"No. Me lovely."

This was the beginning of a relationship that ended up in making Annie a Bottomless. After her accident, she had examined herself in a mirror and concluded that no man in his right frame of mind would want to marry a creature like her. So she had given up ever getting married. And then came Steve. At first she thought he had decided to come round to her place in sympathy of her misfortune. But he kept coming and encouraging her until one day, she tripped over his kiss. And it was a very warm kiss, exuding a lot of sincerity and love. She had not had such a kiss for a long, long time. She fell over and the relationship burnt on. When Steve came to propose, she looked at him with eyes burning with love and told him:

"I can't marry you Steve."

"You can't marry me?" Steve asked desperately.

"No, Steve."

"No! But why? I think I can see love burning in your eyes. Love for no-one else but me. So Annie why won't you marry me?"

"It's true I have a soft spot for you. It's true I love you but ..."

"But what? Annie, I don't want to hear any buts."

"Well, Steve, but I've got the virus."

"The virus! What virus?"

"HIV."

"HHHH IIII VVVV?"

"Yes."

"I get your point. But why should it stand between us?"

"For the obvious reasons."

"Are you telling me that HIV is more powerful than love."

"That's the believe. Test for HIV before you decide to get married. The prospects of many a couple have been shattered."

"Annie, let the entire world believe what they believe. I Steve Bottomless believe in love and love is a bulldozer. The only bulldozer that bulldozes everything in its path, including HIV, AIDS and all. Annie if your but... is HIV, then stand up and give me a fabulous kiss for I can't undo the love I've so painstakingly built up for you."

Steve looked so determined and the love in his eyes so persuasive that Annie couldn't help but stand up and melt in his arms, which culminated in a long, long kiss. When she regained her solidity, Annie looked at Steve straight into his eyes and remarked:

"So my negative HIV status doesn't mean anything to you!"

"Absolutely nothing my love. Nothing. I love you and I shall continue to, in spite of your one thousand and one negative circumstances," Steve said with much conviction.

"The couple took their marriage vows the following week and were very determined to live with HIV and all its consequences," Tom said.

"Have they had any children?" Dion asked.

"They had not considered children as part of their happiness as a couple but they decided to take up the challenge of having them, just to brave the storm of HIV. They've got two healthy kids. A boy and a girl. They are three and five respectively."

"Tom, I find it difficult to comprehend the idea that Steve and Annie could stare such a monster with no qualms and then go ahead and do the things that came from the depths of their hearts. Ndutu couldn't do the same and neither could Jojo. Poor souls, their deaths were unjustified."

"It is simply a question of attitude. The attitude to adopt, in the face of a given situation. When you lost your amulet, you were all panic and confusion, but when I had my epileptic fits you had the presence of mind to dial 999. A gesture that saved my life. Who knows, if the attitude were otherwise, I would have been dumped into the lake like what my dog did to your amulet. My death would have been unjustified. From the little I know about your people, they are very warm and humane but so unsure about the future that they are overwhelmed by uncertainty. They're uncertain about their very existence, so they get into a bizarre practice called witchcraft."

"But Tom, this bizarre practice had existed here."

"Thank God you say *had* existed. It ceased to exist here, hundreds of years ago. Today it is still practised in your country. I used to hear strange things like someone's elephant had been shot in the forest and back in the village the person was dying until they confessed and a ritual was performed to prevent death. People were said to have different animals in them, to ensure their survival. They used to tell me that the rifle, telephone, aeroplane, radio and lots of other western wonders were evidence of the white man's witchcraft. Unfortunately, I had no time to explain the science of the so-called wonders. I'm sure they would marvel more with space exploration and the advent of information super highway. I think, Dion, that this uncertainty is caused by extreme parochialism. The common good isn't much of their concern. Therefore the fear of *what happens to me when I die* is so strong, even though the way of life of your people, as far as I know, is full of optimism. The fear of losing out in the raging war for existence is very strong among them. I remember one man that I met at Fang. He had four wives and each wife had at least three children. When I asked him why that mass acquisition of children, he replied that it was because he personally wanted to ensure continuity. If there were an epidemy, at least one of them would survive. This fear is affecting many aspects of the life of your people. No one would sacrifice so as to ensure the continuity of a community, everyone tries only to take a personal advantage of a common disaster. I remember how drunk an entire village was after a lorry carrying beer had an accident, a kilometre away. Everyone rushed to the scene to grab some bottles of beer for themselves. There was this pathetic case of a car that upturned along one of the highways. I and one other British soldier arrived at the scene two hours after and rescued the victims. We asked if ever since the accident occurred, there hadn't been any vehicles which had passed along the road. They said five passenger buses and three small cars had passed by but they couldn't stop. This gave me the feeling your people are warm only for parochial reasons. Because Ndutu was uncertain about Jojo's reaction to HIV, he kept it to himself and the same goes for Jojo who thought silence and eventual suicide was a better solution for a problem as severe as HIV/AIDS. And I don't mind telling you, Dion, the same fear led you to saddling yourself with a worthless amulet."

"No, no, no Tom. It wasn't worthless. It might have become worthless only after your dog had raped it."

"All right, all right but fear, the fear of uncertainty pushed you to the culture of the amulet. This is what Bertrand Russell, an English gentleman whom I admire so much said about fear: *It is the main source of superstition, and one of the main sources of cruelty. To conquer fear is the beginning of wisdom.*

So Dion, you see the secret of the wonderful exploit of Steve and Annie. I told you they were still alive and they live in Kenilworth."

"I look forward to visiting them."

"Never mind. I'll arrange that," Tom said with much enthusiasm.

"Tell you what Tom, at one point in my life, I did realise that different places had their different climates and the life of the people is influenced by their climates. But I have also come to realise that we all live on the same planet and what is common to all of us is life and death. You might have conquered fear and this is helping you forge ahead fearlessly. It will be good for us too to conquer it and be able to master our paths of life and eventually know what peace really is. I can understand what peace there may be in your getting married to Lisa Armstrad, in anyone staying committed to what they cherish and love, in anyone having as few children as possible to raise, in anyone accepting calamities like HIV/AIDS and living through or with them, in anyone having a choice to or not to act on their overwhelming desires. But what I don't understand is what peace there may be in belonging to a gay club and eventually contracting marriages between *a bone* and *a bone*, and *flesh* and *flesh*.?"

"I get your point, Dion. What you ask is very pertinent and it proves the difference between where you come from and where I come from. The gay issue is rife here because of our tolerant attitudes. It was one of my countrymen George Bernard Shaw who said: *Though all society is founded on intolerance, all improvement is founded on tolerance.* It is because we tolerate one another that there has been great improvement in the world in which we live today. Because of tolerance, people have dared so many things, including the gay issue you've raised. If striving for peace is anyone's goal, there's peace only in doing the right. When you dare and do the wrong, you'll not find the peace you need. So you'll be obliged to do the right. My dear boy, peace, inner peace conquers all, including fear and death."

Dion nodded several times. The old man had just said some very pertinent things. One finds peace only by doing the right. If anything one does is not right there is no way to find peace. He remembered a friend of his who had gone abroad and returned after three years with qualifications in medicine. He soon assumed the title doctor and shortly after he was employed as a medical officer. Dion sensed that there was something not quite right with his achievements and he tried to talk him out of it but the friend rather became hostile. All Dion could do was avoid him. It did not take two years before the police started looking into his qualifications. Since then he had not found peace. He had been on the run and his whereabouts unknown to Dion till date. The old man had also said that peace was all conquering. It conquers both fear and death – the greatest enemies of existence. Peace, especially with oneself must be the most precious possession, which can be found only by doing the right. "But how can we do the right consistently?" Dion wondered.

"Tell me Tom, how can one do the right consistently," he pursued.

Tom looked at Dion intensely, and said, "it is not a question of being consistent in doing the right things but being aware that some of the things you do are wrong and you try to correct them. I'll tell you something. I've been a gay myself. I had no sensual attraction towards women and in fact I still don't have. My desires have been for young stout men like you and I did everything to have them. At one point, I had considered the possibility of becoming a transsexual. Somehow, I realised that it was an improper desire and I thought I should control myself. The fight for self-control was so furious that I actually turned to God. God to me is simply 'Good' short of one of the letters o. Anything good is obviously right. I threw all my worries upon Him in fervent prayer in the hope that he cares and so would provide me with the possibility to surmount my compelling desires. Eventually my prayers paid off and God's book – the bible, became my companion. Later I met Lisa and I married her," Tom said laughing.

Dion looked at Tom, shook his head and made the sign of the cross. He would have been his prey had he not turned to God to suppress his impudent desire. He sat quietly for some time and then thought aloud: "So murderers, burglars, marauders, rapists, pedophilias, crooks and the rest of them who make living on earth a hell can turn around and say: *what I'm doing is wrong*? Peace is not only found in what's right but also in relating fervently to your God, whatever you conceive him to be."

*D*ion Ekpochaba returned to his room forty, Tocil flats more deflated than inflated. Deflated because so far, Tom Jones and his country have impressed him but nothing about his country seemed to have impressed Tom, apart from Tole Tea of course, which he simply discovered by mere chance. He had liked the tea but of what use is it to like something you cannot have or find anywhere? His amulet was looked upon as ridiculous and then the infamous story of Lake Nyos was bad news and then the HIV/AIDS experience was not good either. He thinks our approach to it is rather primitive. Dion racked his brain in search of an impressive story about his country, which he would wish to tell in case a third visit to TJ came up. And it sure would because of the idea of the visit to the Bottomlesses.

Finally, an idea struck him that he should talk about democracy in his country. After all, like capitalism, democracy has conquered the world. And every fair-minded English man and woman would like to hear how democracy was fairing in Cameroon, part of which was their colonial booty. Incidentally, the Germans who had preceded them in colonizing Cameroon were breaking down the Berlin wall in order to take both democracy and capitalism to the East of their Country. Back in Dion's country, Cameroonians were still enjoying their one-party democracy which a *God-sent* president had given them on a platter of gold. People who had hitherto been stifled by a totalitarian leader who ruled them for over two decades were really relishing the trappings of democracy – freedom of expression, universal suffrage, and non-abuse of human rights. Everybody belonged to the party whose name had moved from the People's Union to the People's Movement. It was a real movement of the people, which had become the talk of the day. Nobody wanted to be left behind from the top civil servant to the peasant farmer. There were all types of wings, including a baby wing of the party. No sooner had the people become pleasantly used to this way of life than bells started tolling all over the place, calling for some strange thing called multi-party democracy. It was not really strange as such, because it had been practised before in both East and West of the country but as the dictator did not find such disorder comfortable enough, he banned all the parties and created the People's Union whose activities helped to obliterate any existing memories of the multi-party days.

As expected the barons of the People's Movement were scandalized when calls for multi-party democracy were echoing from across the seas. They wondered how anything could be better than the Movement. They organized marches in all the cities calling for immediate stop of the noise about multi-party democracy. Unfortunately, it was not just noise but a strong wind that was blowing across every single country. Military as well as one party regimes were being looked upon as oppressive and anti-progress. So they deserved nothing other than a crucial crushing. So hardly had the marches stopped than the great leader of the Movement announced the introduction of multi-party democracy. The zealots of the Movement thought that their leader might have gone out of his mind and even suspected foul play. Willy-nilly they came to terms with the reality – multi-party democracy had come to stay. Fortunately for them, however, the Movement remained intact, tall and strong – being the movement of all the people. A few people who had some disaffection with it decided to step aside and form their own parties. Dion found them ridiculous, wondering how they would go into competition with a movement of all the people. Come to think of it, all the disaffected people had their different stances and so formed their different parties, over two hundred in number. Some of whose membership was limited to the immediate and extended family. Dion did not doubt that the disaffected people would end up being disaffected with themselves and their nation because all of them put together would still not be a match to the Movement, a highly entrenched party with the bulldozing machinery of a ruling party.

Dion was quick to realise that if he brought this aspect up in a meeting with TJ, it would be another subject of ridicule. Fortunately for him, there was a sports programme on TV talking about football and the nations which had qualified for the Italia 90 world cup jamboree. His country had qualified and it was one of the only two African countries that had qualified for the competition. That would be a very positive thing to talk about. Dion had always looked on football as battle grounds for people to settle scores. While in primary school there had always existed a cold war between his school, the Presbyterian Boys School and the Saint Philomena School run by the Roman Catholic Mission. Young as they were, pupils of both schools hardly relented in unleashing a war of words at one another, whenever and wherever an opportunity presented itself. So that any day the two schools had to meet in a football match, it was total declaration of war. Agreed that it was only a game, the belligerents who fortunately numbered only eleven on each side, took it so seriously that by the time the referee sounded the final whistle, many of them were rendered as casualties of extreme brutality. Even some supporters who came to relish the pleasure of watching a game, went back home with bleeding heads and noses. At the end of each game the vanquished are subdued waiting broodingly for a time to revenge. The game was rather a way of expressing ill-will and using the opportunity to dissipate the fierce combative tendencies in both the players and the spectators.

Dion was therefore all pride and boastfulness when his country was one of the only two countries from the vast continent of Africa to qualify for the world cup. Providence had made it that Cameroon would play the opening match against an almighty Argentinian football team, the current world champions.

Before the match, most people Dion talked to gave the match to Argentina and all his African friends who were not Cameroonians found it ridiculous when he boasted that Cameroon was going to carry the day.

"That's being ridiculously patriotic," one of them said. "How can you think that your little known country will beat Argentina in the game of football, with Diego Maradona as the captain? What you should hope for is a mild score of six goals to zero," he pursued.

"That's our greatest problem, we Africans," Dion said. "We hardly believe in ourselves. What miracle is there in beating Argentina? All it takes is eleven determined men who believe in themselves and what they're doing. Had David not believed in himself how would he have beaten Goliath in battle?" Dion pursued.

"Young man, David was inspired by God," he said mockingly.

"The same God can inspire the Cameroonian team," Dion said resolutely.

"That's all right. Let's wait and see".

"I can't wait to see the lions devour the Argentinians," Dion said provocatively.

Somehow Dion felt so confident about the team from his homeland. It had not been long since he left home and he had been very impressed with the performances of all the players in the team. He knew all of them by name and also what they were capable of. He regretted that he did not have enough money to travel to Italy to watch them live. Nevertheless, thanks to cable television they could be watched live at any corner of the world. So on the day of the match he sat with other students in the airport lounge - that's how the hall of the Student Union building at the university was called. Being a world cup opening match, there was so much ceremony. Eyes were glued on the giant screen, expecting to watch the exploits of Maradona and his teammates. Nobody but him gave a thought to the other team. His African friends who had thought he was being too patriotic to think that his country would win the match had decided they would not watch it. They had concluded that it was one too many an opportunity to humiliate the African continent. The TV Camera zoomed past the president of my country sitting proudly in the tribune where only the who is who in the world sat. He found it reassuring and he continued to watch. Finally, the team officials walked into the playground, followed by the players of the two teams. Diego Maradonna, the man everyone wanted to see came in amid loud applause. Fans screamed and cheered and he on his part played all types of tricks with the ball. He juggled the ball on his shoulders head, back and heels. Dion felt very intimidated but when the captain of the lions, Tataw Etah Stephen stood face to face with Maradona, he was relieved. He was many centimetres taller and even looked broader than the world's best footballer. Dion knew he was going to handle him appropriately to let the world know that he too existed. Then it was kick off and the minutes started ticking away. After fifteen minutes of the game, a blonde sitting by Dion asked him where he came from. He smiled and articulated the name Cameroon. The blonde turned and looked at him curiously and asked:

"How did they learn to play football so well?"

"It's simply in their blood. King Pele of Brazil originated from there," Dion said proudly.

"I believe you. I can see it in the way they twist, turn, kick and tackle. I bet they might even carry the day."

"They sure will," said Dion confidently.

The half ended no goal on either side. During half time, he noticed that he was attracting a lot of attention. He was the only black face in the lounge and every one in the hall wanted to know where those great ball jugglers came from. By the time the second half started Dion no longer felt ignored. The goals they were all waiting for from the Argentinians did not come and so many of them switched camps and began to expect goals from the Cameroonian team. Suddenly, there was so much excitement as a certain Canniga raised towards the Cameroonian goal. Before he could put the excellent goalkeeper to test, he was heavily brought down and the referee was only too glad to offer the champions a free kick and expel the player with a show of the red card. Minutes later, another red card and the team were down by two men. The champions had an added luxury of playing against a diminutive team of nine men whose morale had been broken by the expulsions. The champions gained in confidence and were very hopeful that they would carry the day. Diego Maradona was all over the place to prove that he was the world's best. Hard as he tried, his efforts were thwarted by captain Tataw and a vibrant Ndip Akem Victor. And then there was this kick that met Omam Biyick at the left post. He literally flew into the air above the struggling Argentinian defenders and placed his head forcefully on the ball. The goalkeeper went for it and caught it but it slipped through his fingers and rolled lazily across the goal line. It was a goal. Dion could not help screaming: a David has come to prove his worth! The lounge went wild with excitement and suddenly Dion was receiving hugs from all sides. When the ball was taken to the centre for a restart, the Argentinians and their fans knew they had business with a very hard nut to crack. They became very desperate, which only eroded their fortunes. At the blast of the final whistle Dion had become a hero. A hitherto unknown quantity had become a much–sought-after personality for autographs.

rue to the thought of Irving Berlin, *the toughest thing about success is that you've got to keep on being a success,* Dion was haunted by the expectations of his new found fans. They all had high hopes for the Cameroonian team, which they agreed deserved the name indomitable lions. Fellow Africans who had been doubting Thomases went back to him to apologise and congratulate him and his country on making Africa proud. They said they had not imagined that an African country could be capable of such an exploit – to humiliate the world's best in the full glare of billions of eyes. Dion's greatest headache was to contain these fans and possibly sustain them. In this regard he was more anxious about the outcome of the subsequent matches. His friend TJ could not help ringing him up the following day:

"Hello Dion, it's nice to have you on the line. I've been dying to talk to you."

"What about?"

"Your country! The football team has done great. In fact they have conquered the world."

"I didn't know you were a football fan, Tom."

"Yes I am. If you didn't know, Stanley Matthews was my cousin and besides I'm even more excited because of my relationship with your country and of course with you."

"Glad to hear that."

"I really enjoyed your team. They were brilliant. There was that M-a-k-a-n-a boy."

"You mean Makanaky."

"Yes Makanaky. That's the name. In my opinion, he was more than Maradona in the game. He could do all kinds of foot tricks with the ball. And then the young man who did it all. It was a great leap. He leaped above everyone else and placed his head on the ball. The header was too strong for the poor goalkeeper. That one, what's his name? O-oman Bi-ik."

"Omam Biyick. That's the name."

"That's right, Omam not Oman. And then there was the Massing boy manhandled the entire Argentinian attack. It was real fun watching a mélange of art and brutality. "

"I'm so pleased something about my country made you so happy."

"It sure did and I hope to follow them up until the end of the competition. I'm so proud I know you and I'm dying to introduce you to everyone I know. So tell me, when next shall we meet? Remember I have to take you to the Bottomlesses."

"I sure do."

"Talk to you later, bye."

"Bye."

Dion looked forward to the second match, hoping the team had not dissipated all the energy they had to humiliate the world champions. So, on the day the lions marched to the football arena waiting to devour Haji and his teammates from Romania, Dion silently prayed for the lion's success. He was the centre of attraction and more and more autograph seekers came to him. When the match started, the confidence that radiated from the players built up his own confidence. They played like masters of the game and at one point they introduced their trump card – Roger Milla, a thirty-eight-year-old attacker. He had had a world cup experience eight years earlier when Cameroon first participated in the competition. Roger Milla got on the pitch and became a sensation. He made the Romanian goalkeeper turn around grudgingly to pick up the ball at the back of his net twice. The two goals gave Cameroon another victory and the first team in the competition to qualify for the eighth finals. And so the success was sustained. The third group match was a nonevent as the players were more concerned with crushing whoever were to be their opponents at the eighth finals. The celebrity status of Dion was improving everyday. He had to receive as many as two hundred students each day. They wanted to associate with a winning side. They asked all sorts of questions about his country, which had become a dreamland for many of them. He hardly found time to arrange an appointment with his friend Tom Jones. Then came the day of the eighth final game, which was against a crack Colombian side, whose attack force was led by a certain Valderama, rated as a deadly striker. Thankfully, the Cameroonian team had since learnt not to worship idols. The match came on and again Roger Milla did the magic. He spiced the match with a special goal. The legendary Colombian goalkeeper Higuitta had stopped a ball with his right foot. Instead of picking it up or getting rid of it by kicking it forward, he nursed the crazy idea of dribbling Roger Milla. In an attempt to do so, Milla proved to him that he was an old fox in the art of dribbling. He timed his dibble and seized the ball from him. Before Higuitta could come to terms with what had happened, Milla was speeding towards his goal post with the ball firmly on his feet. Higuitta gave a wild chase but too late he couldn't catch up with the fleet footed attacker. Only seconds later the ball was at the back of the net. Poor Higuitta, what he had not known was that Milla had for over two decades been dribbling goalkeepers and not the other way round. He dolefully walked to the back of his net, picked up the ball and lazily rolled it to the centre of the field. That goal gave Cameroon the victory it deserved and the team smiled away to the prestigious quarter final stage of the competition. Who were going to be their opponents? It did not take long to know. England too had qualified for the quarter finals, which was the exclusive preserve of the eight best teams in this big wide world. A sort of G8. Dion was very proud of his country which had suddenly found itself in the prestigious G8 group. A meeting with Tom Jones was quite auspicious.

"Good to see you Dion."

"Good to see you too."

"It's been quite a while. I hear you're so busy taking care of you fans – Dion the lion, the indomitable lion."

"Sure, sure Tom. Every situation has its trappings. I'm struggling to cope with the trappings of celebrity."

111

"I know what it takes. Now, what about dashing to Kenilworth?"

"What's there?"

"The Bottomlesses of course."

"Ok! Let's."

In under twenty minutes they were at the doorbell of the Bottomlesses. As soon as the door opened and a woman with a mellifluous voice asked them in, Dion knew that was Annie. Shortly after, Steve appeared.

"Hello, you must be Dion. I'm Steve and this is my wife Annie."

"My pleasure to meet you both for the first time."

"Our pleasure too," chorused the couple.

"And you Tom, how are doing?" Steve said.

"Oh, not bad," answered Tom.

"Do sit down. Dion we hear you're from Cameroon, the African country that's doing extremely well at the ongoing world cup competition."

"Yes, I am."

"How do you feel about your country's performance?"

"I feel great."

"Glad to hear that. And your next victim will be England."

"Why do you say victim."

"Because you're on a winning streak. You crush every single opponent. I have a feeling this is Africa's turn to take the trophy."

"I have the same feeling too. I don't see how we shouldn't take the trophy after we had beaten the current champions."

"Do you mean your team will beat England?"

"They can't possibly be taking the world cup without beating their next opponent," Dion said with much conviction.

"Don't be so sure. Football is an English invention."

"Therefore England should consistently be champions," Dion said flatly.

"I get what you mean. We've been champions only once. The last time we hosted the competition. But Dion your country's fairytale will end on the day of the quarter finals."

"Tom, I'm surprised, you call our exploits a fairytale. I thought you were one of those who admired and encouraged what we were doing?"

"I did admire your exploits when it had to do with outsiders but when it has to do with England you can be sure where my sympathies will go. Because of England I braved the scorching heat in your country. Because of England I have taken so many risks and so because of England I would disavow my admiration for devouring lions. I shall hate to see them devour England."

"But football is only a game. You can't talk about it so seriously," Annie said.

"It's more than just a game. It's a question of prestige, which has to be fought for ferociously. You get disgraced if you lose, so you must fight to win. Worst of all, to lose to a country like Dion's. I

113

hope you understand what I mean. England must do its utmost to win."

"I understand you, but in my opinion game arenas should not be turned into battlefields because we must win at all cost," Annie said.

"I do agree with Annie," Steve said.

"That's understandable. You both never experienced the empire days." Tom Jones said.

Annie Bottomless brought in some tea and cookies and we treated ourselves to each a cup. The couple was very relaxed and they did not seem to carry any burden. Their daughter and son were both love and vitality. No sign of discomfort anywhere. Before they separated they had agreed to watch the match together in Kenilworth.

It was a warm summer day when they gathered in the home of the Bottomlesses. Dion had excused himself from his fans who had insisted that they watched the match at the airport lounge. Dion's excuse was only accepted because he had lied to them that he was travelling to London to watch the match with a Cameroonian community there. Annie and Steve were very dependable hosts. We had a very exciting conversation before the match started. The game was as exciting as the previous ones. When England scored the first goal, Annie and Steve did not look too happy but Tom, in spite of his age shot both hands up cheering and cheering the goal. Dion's spirits dampened and he was glad he had stayed away from the airport lounge. He did not, however, give up hopes. The match went on intensely and the indomitable lions got the equalizer. He jumped up so high, his head almost touched the ceiling. Poor Tom, he looked so low that I feared he might get into a fit. Things got worse for him when Eugene Ekeke slammed in the second goal.

The electronic board read Cameroon 2 - England 1. Dion could not hold back the tears that surprised him - tears of joy. Then, in spite of himself, he began singing loud and clear:

O Cameroon, thou cradle of our fathers
Holy shrine where in thy midst they now repose…
… … … … … … … … …
Land of promise, land of glory
And deep endearment, forever more.

The others looked at him in amazement Annie could not help asking:

"Hey Dion, what's that song supposed to be? It sounds beautiful."

"Yeah, it is. It's my country's anthem, the national anthem. Supposed to be sung in times of glory. We are experiencing one of such times in this room."

"I'm happy for you Dion," said Annie.

"So you should Annie. At this moment I can visualize the Greyell star fluttering above the Union jack."

"And what's the Greyell star?"

"Dear me, I've got a lot of explaining to do today. Anyway the Greyell star is my country's flag. It's got green, red and yellow colours, with a star in the middle. So we call it the Greyell star as you call yours the Union jack and the French call theirs Tricolor. As I was saying the Greyell star is at this moment fluttering above the Union jack.

And so Cameroon led England as the minutes were ticking away very fast. Tom's age suddenly got a grip on him as he could not even get out of his chair when he felt like going to ease himself. Steve Bottomless had to support him. When he returned to his seat, there were only ten minutes left for the final whistle. I was looking forward to a great fall. Another fall of the Empire. But seven minutes to go the referee knew what to do. He awarded England, the inventors of the game, a penalty and Gary whom the English graciously called Lion-leaker converted it into a goal. Shortly after, the referee invented another penalty for the game's inventors. Again the Lion-leaker carried out his function and so shattered the vibrancy and aspirations of the indomitable lions. As I sat there, I watched the castles I had built in the air collapse one after the other. Tom Jones suddenly sat up, his strength had returned miraculously and he started singing *God save the Queen*. As his eyes were still on the screen he turned and asked: "What's going on? It's rather the Cameroonians who are jubilating on the field, running round and waving to the crowd. Do you now celebrate defeat in your country?"

"Depends on what you mean by defeat."

"Losing in a war or in a competition. Your country has just suffered one, Dion."

"So you expected the players to be weeping and complaining on the pitch? They've come a long way, Tom. They've learnt not to panic even after their amulet has been raped."

The Bottomlesses were a very nice family. They understood how Dion felt at the end of the

116

day and they did all they could to make him happy. Annie and the children kissed him goodbye when Steve offered to drive him and Tom Jones back home. Tom was dropped off at Cannon park and Dion was taken to the University campus. He was very silent most of the way, wondering at what awaited him on his arrival, at number 40, Tocil flats.